# Redcoat 1812

*a novel by*

## *John Nixon*

Published by:

FriesenPress
Suite 300 – 852 Fort Street
Victoria, BC, Canada V8W 1H8

www.friesenpress.com

Distributed to the trade by The Ingram Book Company

*For Barbara*

# 1
## *Ireland, 1798*

Despite my protestations I knew, even then, I'd never see Ireland again.

To the beat of the drum we marched through Glin, behind soldiers in scarlet tunics, off to Limerick and ships that would take us only God knew where. Keeping our thoughts to ourselves, wondering if we were in for better fortune than our homeland promised, we took one last look at the sad little village of our boyhood. Few bystanders even bothered to stop what they were doing to see who else was joining the exodus from Ireland. If they did glance up it was easy enough to read the expression on their faces: Foolish you are to leave, foolish to stay, foolish no matter what you do.

Ireland was fertile ground for the British army, and the recruiting sergeants knew just where to go to dig up soldiers. They'd go straight to the places where desperate young men congregate: outside the ale house where they'd be hoping someone might buy them a drink, or down at the church, standing in line waiting their turn for a hot bowl of soup. The priest might chase the army men away from outside the church, but they'd be back the next day. Persistent buggers. And good at chattin' up the lads they were. Five minutes with them and taking the King's shilling for seven years of danger seemed like a fair trade. Of course idle young men wanting to spend the shilling on drink and a full belly aren't always thinking too clearly.

The 49th never had difficulty enlisting men. Their regimental colour was green. The green facing on the scarlet tunics and the green tuft of feathers on the black, felt shako cap appealed to Irishmen, and that was good enough reason to pick a unit. Wanting to meet their quota, the recruiters rarely turned anyone away. The lads often joked that the only requirement to join the British army was to have enough teeth in your head to tear open the paper cartridge holding the powder and ball for your musket.

Most of the recruits had few choices, but my situation was different. As we marched my thoughts drifted back to the day before, when I told my parents of my decision. I'd been sitting in my usual place, at the table in our stone cottage, with one of my precious books open in front of me, trying not to think about the aroma of the gorgeous fresh bread on the table not two feet away. The book was open, but I wasn't bothering with it. I was watching Mam as she busied herself with supper. Cleverly she was tossing mysterious ingredients into the giant black soup kettle hanging in the fireplace, and stirring her creation with a ladle that released more delicious smells into the room made warm by the fire. Every movement was deliberate. Every action purposeful. She was lean from years of hard women's work. Fighting trim I'd say, so long as she couldn't hear me. It wasn't difficult to imagine the beautiful colleen who had her pick of suitors not that many years ago, but the lines were starting to show on her face and there was more grey hiding in her luxurious chestnut hair than she'd want us to notice. No stranger to disappointment was my Mam. Her only indulgence was the red ribbon holding back that hair.

I had waited until my Da came into the cottage. Didn't want to have to do this twice. He'd been seeding the last field and tending our livestock. Sheep, a few dairy cows, and pigs there were. Da wiped his brow with a handkerchief and poured himself a cup of cool water from the pitcher on the table. As he drank his water he looked my way and smiled. It was then that I carefully took the shilling from my pocket and placed it on the table, loudly enough for both of them to notice. For a solitary moment there was no sound in the cottage except the crackling of the fire beneath the soup. Da stared not at me, but at the coin. Mam's back had been to me. Slowly she turned, glanced at the coin, and looked me straight in the eye.

"James FitzGibbon, you stupid boy, what have you gone and done? You're educated. You've prospects. It was only last week the squire was asking your father about you. He'll be seeking an overseer for his estate soon enough. That position could be yours!"

I'd been collecting my thoughts for awhile. Pointing to the book in front of me I said, "Mam, you shouldn't have given me all these books to read if you didn't want me to go off and see the world for myself. I won't be happy managing the squire's estate for the rest of my life."

Incredulous she was. Mam looked at her husband. "Happiness he wants!"

But Da was looking at the floor with resignation. It had been daft to enroll my brother John and me in the local militia to defend beloved Ireland from Napoleon, as though the Frenchie might go mad one day and covet our God-forsaken little village more than anything else in the world. He knew that I'd taken to the military life, more than he wanted.

Getting no response from my father, Mam went on. I hadn't expected her to give in readily. "Most of the village lads would give an arm for a splendid, freehold property like this. What will happen to our farm? How will we manage?"

"There's not enough farm to keep both John and me. By rights, he's the eldest and it'll all be his one day. Besides he's better suited to it. One day one of us will be leavin'. Would you rather be waving to him as he marches off? I've been the drilling sergeant for the militia unit since I was fifteen. And I still need to keep John from harm when he's loading his musket."

"You'll be a common soldier then?"

"No, they've offered me a sergeant's pay."

"You're only eighteen, couldn't you stay here awhile longer, boy?"

As gently as I could I said, "Mam, you know yourself what would happen. In no time at all I'd be bored, and up to some mischief. There'd be some dour man, ledger in hand, knocking on your door wanting to have a quiet word with you about the money I owed him. Or some angry father banging on the door in the middle of the night wanting to have not so quiet a word with your wayward son about his daughter."

Shaking her head in exasperation she asked, "Must you join the British army? The English are responsible for half of Ireland's troubles."

"What other army would I join? Would you rather see me sneaking off each night to some secret meeting and plotting to free Ireland, hoping that the King's men didn't catch me at it?"

Finally, she got to the thing on her mind that worried her the most. "You might be killed."

Before answering I paused to show I given this careful consideration, then said, "God numbers all of our days." Being a good Catholic woman, I knew she wouldn't disagree with this.

Da, who had said nothing 'til now, looked lovingly at Mam. "James enlisting, perhaps it's for the best. We'll manage somehow."

Turning back toward me, Mam whispered, as much to herself as to me, "I may never see you again."

"Of course you will. I'll just be off for a short while. I'll straighten out the English army, learn a little French, and return a better man. It'll be grand. Maybe I'll meet Napoleon himself and tell him about your soup."

She snorted.

"Should I bring something back for you?" I asked.

She replied, "Just yourself in good health, and some of your fanciful tales".

Then I saw something I'd never seen before. In the eye of the woman who had stood resolute against whatever life handed her, there was a tear. I watched as Mam moved closer to where I was seated. She hesitated, and gently whacked me on my arm with her ladle.

# 2
## *Holland, 1799*

After a year of incessant drilling and endless preparation for battle, the 49th finally received its orders. We were crammed onto ships and transported across the English Channel to the continent. To Holland, a place called Egmont-op-Zee, we were told, although it mattered little to us where we were. Small boats carried us to the sandy beach. We were damp with spray and shivered in the chill morning air. The nasty, overcast sky affected our disposition. The lads joked that it was a lovely English day. We fully expected French troops to be there to greet us, but they'd missed their opportunity.

On the beach we formed up. Flags were unfurled; the Union Jack and our regimental colours fluttered in the breeze. The drum beat instructed us. Orders were shouted. Men moved in unison. The atmosphere was exhilarating. This was our first chance to be soldiers.

We marched up the sand hills at the end of the beach to the wind-blown field at the top to join the other British regiments. There we were positioned in the standard three-line battle formation. The first two lines were firing lines, one line always loading muskets while the other was firing, which minimized time between volleys. The men in the third were the replacements for the casualties; as men fell, they dragged the dead and wounded back and took their place. Loading a musket is trickier than it looks. It requires calm, co-ordinated movements: butt on the ground, cartridge from the pouch, teeth tearing paper, powder in the pan, cover over the pan, ball and powder in the barrel, ramrod out, rod down the barrel, rod back in place, musket to shoulder, flintlock cocked, and trigger pulled. Three times a minute was a rate to be proud of, and that we were now capable of doing.

On our side of the field there were flaming red jackets as far as the eye could see, the long lines spreading in both directions. Red, blue, yellow and buff flags, as well as our green, were behind them. Cavalry units darted by to their position on one end. Artillery caissons pulled by straining horses clattered past us to the other. Through the grey morning light across the field, we could make out long blue lines of men, as anxious for the battle to begin as we were.

A musket battle is one monstrous duel. It isn't two dandies pacing off twelve steps, firing at their foe to impress some lady or address some grievance, then getting back in their carriage and driving off looking for a drink and a warm fire. Not so bloody civilized. It's hundreds, maybe thousands of men, admittedly further apart, shooting constantly at one another while they stand in place until one side loses its nerve and bolts for cover, or none of them are left standing. With a musket a soldier can't hit a barn door at sixty yards. Too much aiming is pointless. But grand volleys, sending more lead balls than a man could count in the same direction, can do some damage. We'd heard that the new rifles were more accurate, but often jammed and wouldn't take a bayonet, so muskets it was.

As far as we were concerned, the splendid schemes of generals were well and good, but it was the bravery of the men in line that won battles and wars. In duels it's all about honour and not being afraid. Standing perfectly still in a bright coloured jacket and shiny brass buckles while some bugger tries to kill you is mad, if you think about it. What man with a brain in his head wouldn't be afraid? The secret is not thinking about it. Concentrate on the task at hand, don't feel anything at all, load your musket as calmly possible, follow orders, and never panic. Nothing else. Don't be lookin' at the man lying on the ground beside you. Don't be listening to the groans of the wounded. Redcoats are invincible. That's what we'd been told. That's what was drilled into our heads. And we'd better not be forgetting it.

While we were waiting, I wandered about, chattering away, trying to distract my men. "Isn't this just what that lovely recruiting sergeant promised you? A chance to visit amazing and wonderful lands. Warmer days than you'd ever find in Ireland. Marvellous adventures."

One lad shouted back, "That was the most glorious beach I'd ever seen."

Another asked, "When do we get to see the gorgeous French countryside, Sergeant?"

I answered, "Soon enough lads. The Frenchies over there are standing in our way. We'll be asking them to step aside. Surely they'll appreciate our good manners and do as we ask."

Just then our commanding officer rode up to wish us well. I'd only seen him from a distance before. Up close I got a better view. He had an athletic build . He was a large man, more than six foot, although difficult to say how much more as he was sitting in a saddle. I'm sure the ladies would say he was dashing—dashing enough anyway.

Enjoying himself he was; his expression gave him away. His uniform was immaculate. What caught my attention though was the green scarf wound tightly around his neck. Perhaps for warmth, perhaps for fashion.  Probably silk, although I'd not seen enough of that material to know. Not regulation, but I didn't know who would be bold enough to be tellin' him. He rode down the line saying, " Do your best men. You're better soldiers than they are. Never think you're not. The regiment and I are counting on you." Then much to our surprise, he didn't gallop off to some secure place behind, but reigned up his horse, stopped, and waited with us.

There was a moment of ominous silence, then commands were given, repeated up and down the line by junior officers. "Load......... First line...... Aim......... Fire." A menacing, deafening explosion of a thousand muskets followed. Smoke swirled. The acrid smell of gunpowder filled the air. My eyes stung.

Then came the French reply. A few men in the unit crumpled, dead before they hit the ground. Anguished cries came from the wounded as musket balls penetrated limbs, stomachs, heads. Cannon thundered in the distance. From our officers: "Second line..... Aim........ Fire." With deft movement the fallen were pulled back. We sergeants used our pikes to direct third liners into place. As we exchanged volleys, the noise grew louder. There was so much smoke that truth be told, we wouldn't recognize our mothers at twenty paces if they'd been aiding the French. Musket barrels heated. Some jammed. We fired not at three times a minute now, only two. In the midst of this I saw the head of our commander snap back. Then he came forward, struggling to steady himself by grasping the neck of his horse, but slowly he slid from the animal onto the ground and lay on his back. I rushed to his assistance, calling as I went, "Surgeon! Surgeon! You are needed here." I kept repeating this until our regimental physician, an older, mustachioed officer, appeared. He examined the Lieutenant-Colonel.

There was no blood seeping out. No gaping hole. Still he lay there, motionless, eyes closed.

"Sergeant, help me get this scarf undone," directed the physician. Doing as I had been told, I lifted the head gently and unwound the scarf until the neck could be seen clearly. A broad darkening bruise was apparent. The surgeon bent closer and called his name attempting to raise his consciousness. "Isaac........Brock........Isaac Brock.. Can you hear me?"

At last, eyelids fluttered and he whispered, "Am I hurt?"

"Not that I can see," was the response. "You're a lucky man, Brock. That musket ball must have been fired from some great distance, losing strength as it went. That damned scarf of yours helped as well."

With a shallow voice and a short smile, Brock said to his friend, "Told you. Foolish to go into battle without a scarf." The fellow officer shook his head and directed me further. "Sergeant, take one arm, I'll take the other. We'll get him back to my tent so he may be observed. Bring his horse." I did as instructed, thinking to myself, "Good to be led by a brave and capable man. Better to be led by one who's lucky as well."

Having deposited my charge in the surgeon's tent, I hurried back to my unit. The battle had continued in my absence. There was so much smoke and confusion that I became disoriented and took the wrong path back. As I was about to enter an unfamiliar wood lot, four French soldiers came out. Their muskets were slung on their backs and arms were extended as if they might be seeking surrender. "Halt," I ordered, while affixing my bayonet. The four stopped and starred back in confusion, not understanding my words. They argued back and forth in their strange tongue, and appeared to reach some decision. Quickly they unslung their muskets and pointed them directly at me. Calculating my odds, I concluded that one musket ball and one bayonet were not enough to overcome the four men ready to kill me. Ashamed, I dropped my musket and became their prisoner.

I do not care to recount the embarrassment of my three months of French hospitality until the prisoner exchange. I will only relate three things. First, the only words of French I learned cannot be repeated in fine company. Second, during my enforced idleness there was ample opportunity to review my unfortunate circumstance. I vowed never to forget its lesson. Eyes can be deceived. Things are not always what they seem. And last, nothing in the world is more exhilarating than going into battle. These were things I think I knew all along.

# 3

## *Lower Canada, 1802*

A young lieutenant, barely sixteen I'd wager, strode purpose-fully into our barracks. "We've been ordered to the Canadas. Prepare yourselves to depart in two days." When we didn't supply whatever response he was anticipating, the arrogant sod continued. "They're in the Americas, the northern-most part."

Since the unfortunate campaign in Holland, the 49th had been stationed on Jersey, one of the Channel Islands, amusing ourselves with relentless manoeuvres and awaiting our next posting. Being sent to some distant backwater of the British Empire was less than most of us hoped for. Only those dis-inclined toward any fighting at all were in good spirits after receiving the news. It had been just two decades since revolu-tionaries had defeated His Majesty's army at Yorktown and the Thirteen Colonies had been surrendered. Anyone with ears knew that. Guarding the northern bits of the continent should the Americans, as they were calling themselves now, unexpect-edly change their minds about wanting them, was hardly a preferred assignment. But we kept our thoughts to ourselves. The lieutenant wasn't interested in what we thought.

Two days subsequent, the regiment boarded warships bound for Quebec. Our accommodation was adequate, but only comparing it to other ways of getting there. At home in Ireland, stories of travel to the Canadas were circulating. In the ale houses there'd been tales of 'coffin ships' taking human ballast in their empty holds after depositing timber cargoes in Britain, with passengers paying prices that left little for provisions and cholera thrown in for free. We had no way of knowing if the tales were true, but our passage was much better. The army looked after us. Too many hours and too much money had been spent preparing us to be soldiers. We were too valuable a commodity to be squandered. My only complaint on the journey was a never-ending sea-sickness. Some lads adjusted quickly to the rolling of the sailing ships, but my stomach did as it wished. Each day I prayed, something I did not often do, that my stomach would calm and no storm would overtake us and make my situation worse. Some prayers are not readily answered.

After six weeks with little to observe, land came into view. The tides pulled fresh water from some monstrous river that appeared to be guiding us inland. Most of the regiment gathered on deck to see this unfamiliar country for ourselves. At first, the cliffs were too high to see more than countless seabirds that whorled and dove for dinner, but as the river narrowed and we sailed nearer to shore, much more was revealed. There were narrow strips of cultivated farmland fronting the river. On each strip was a whitewashed, stone farm house and a thatched-roof, wooden barn, presumably for livestock and fodder. Women and children could be seen working in gardens nearer the house. The strips appeared to go considerable distance back from the river. Fields of grain and wood lots could barely be seen. Each farm seemed a self-sufficient endeavour. They were larger, more diverse, and less rectangular than the plots worked by tenant farmers in Glin. If this was what could be expected here, with little encouragement, most Irishmen would take their chances with cholera. Surely the British Isles would empty out.

On what was to be our final day on ship I awoke to some small commotion on deck. I was drawn to the bow with the others to see what had caught their interest. In dawn's pale light, above the mist rising from the river, there was a fortress. A citadel. Dominating. Imposing. Magnificent. It was perched on a rocky escarpment towering over an awakening commercial centre below. Its stone ramparts intimidated and its gun batteries commanded the river. An ancient stronghold. A Scottish officer said that it reminded him of Edinburgh's castle. I had never seen such a sight, and in such an unanticipated place. So this is Quebec, I said to myself. At last we had arrived in the Canadas. Secretly, I hoped to be done with ships forever.

Later that day we disembarked and marched through the lower town, finer than Limerick, along its narrow cobbled streets, through open air plazas, and past fine houses with window boxes and trellises covered in flowers beginning to bloom. Many of the houses were built of stone and two or three stories high. We past enough steepled, Catholic churches to awe my Mam. It was easy enough to imagine her standing there in holy admiration as the priests and nuns bustled about. Up the escarpment we went to the walled town above, passing through fortified gateways to the parade grounds in front of the barracks that were to be our temporary home.

Entering the grounds, we were greeted by our commanding officers, not in a more formal, salute-as-we-pass way as might be expected, but in a more informal, amiable manner. Brock, now a full colonel, showing no ill effects from his injury, stood in front welcoming each company with a spirit of hospitality. Behind him stood the second in command, Lieutenant Colonel Roger Hale Sheaffe. Despite the spelling he pronounced his family name SHAFE, rhyming with safe, and God help the soldier who forgot that. Sheaffe was a hawk-faced man with a malevolent glare, older than Brock, ever vigilant for some transgression from regulations in need of correction. We had learned that nothing pleased him more than bringing an infraction to a soldier's attention. He was the type of officer who demanded respect, presumably to dissuade us from any other inclination. From his demeanor he clearly wished to distance himself from Brock's notion of cordiality.

As my company passed, Colonel Brock recognized me, smiled, and stepped forward. Quickly my men halted. "Sergeant FitzGibbon," said he. "I understand that you came to my assistance in Holland. I wish to thank you." I was taken aback at this courtesy, but endeavoured to continue this conversation. "Glad to be of assistance, Sir. Have you been to the Canadas before, Colonel Brock?" "No Sergeant, I have not. From what I've been told it's too cold in the winter, too hot in the summer, and a long way from Napoleon," he replied. "In time FitzGibbon, perhaps we'll both find it a great deal more than that." Brock then returned to his former position, nodded to me, and raised his voice so the entire company could hear, " What an excellent company this is. Well done." The compliment was much appreciated by the lads.

The regiment spent the remainder of that year and the start of the next at Quebec. There was much to observe and sufficient time to do it. I was most intrigued by the people. Although men of prosperity and influence might be English, the majority of the inhabitants of Quebec and the surrounding area spoke French. They called themselves 'Les Habitants' and sometimes 'Les Canadiens". They were the ones who populated the farms we had seen from the river, and the rest of Lower Canada. They were the ones who lived in Quebec's lower town, working the docks, arranging for the passage of goods, plying their trades, and serving the prosperous. They were the ones who offered delicious soups and breads, jams and cheese for sale from their homes or little shops, and who turned wool and leather into products for purchase. They were the ones we encountered when off-duty and in search of warmer socks, vests, or drink in the lower town. Considering that they admitted to speaking little English, and we did not 'parlez' at all, interactions were cordial enough. There was no malice or animosity in them, but no welcome or friendship either. It was difficult for me to comprehend how England could be fighting the French on one side of the ocean and coexisting with them on the other. I was determined to take every opportunity to learn. Whenever officers or English merchants conversed, I listened. Whenever questions could be asked, I did. Whenever a newspaper could be acquired, I read it. Eventually I came to know something of their story. Their ancestors had settled this land and had been here for generations. Forty years before, the French king had abandoned them and their "few acres of snow" after losing a seven-year war to the English. The English had now come to some arrangement with them. They could keep their language and customs in exchange for loyalty. All they had to do was let the revolutionary fervour of the Americans fall on deaf ears. Having little choice, they had acquiesced. Irishmen understood acquiescence.

The 49th wintered in Quebec, safely stationed in our barracks, with the fortress walls keeping the snow at bay. Then in April of the new year, as my restlessness began to unsettle me, the snow disappeared, the river ice melted, and the passageway inland opened. Without delay we set off up-river for Upper Canada.

# 4

## *Upper Canada, 1803*

The regiment left Quebec in a flotilla of bateaux, the flat bottomed boats much fancied by the army. The boats were more than twenty feet long and propelled by rowers. They had small, squarish sails, should breeze make them useful. Happily we took turns at the oars, an hour at a time, as activity broke the boredom and kept us fit. Only our blistered hands complained. Five days along we reached Montreal, a commercial centre with wharves and storehouses crowding the riverbank. It compared favourably with a middle-sized country town at home. The many whitewashed, stone houses topped with slate or tin roofs suggested prosperity, much like Quebec. Only the doors and windows were different: they were all fitted with iron shutters or bars. I wondered from whom or what the residents needed protection.

After one night's rest in something resembling a bed we set off again, loaded with supplies. Not far along it was necessary to portage the river rapids below Lachine—portage being the lovely French word for getting out of our boats, lifting all our possessions into carts, and walking around the wild bits of the river that might do damage to boats or their occupants. We rowed another ten days along the St. Lawrence, covering eighteen miles a day according to our helmsman, through another four sets of foaming rapids, and skirting primeval forests that were broken occasionally by small clearings where log cabins were situated. The air was brisk and filled with the scent of damp pine. Hoards of geese and ducks flew overhead. They found our presence objectionable, judging by the noise they made. Deer, fox, and other animals I could not name watched from the river bank. Whenever a farmer was burning stumps or brush from his fields, the pungent smell of smoke mingled with the pine. All in all, the scenery would be thought beautiful by anyone who had acquired a great interest in trees.

Next we entered some immense, fresh water lake that was icy cold to the touch. It was inconceivable to me that any lake could be so grand; more like an inland sea it was. Deep enough to hide half a dozen Irish counties. Countless fish could be seen just below the surface. To pass the time we made up stories of lake monsters that might amuse the drinkers in the ale houses of our little county towns. Not long into the lake we approached Kingston, a fortified harbour crammed with sailing vessels. Gun batteries guarded the mouth of the harbour. More cannon were visible on the hilltop fort above. Beside the fortification was a little town, neat and orderly by all appearances. But there was little time to explore. We were transferred onto schooners, two masted sailing ships, which set off into a strong headwind. It took another seven days to cross the lake. As we neared our destination, a rain squall overtook us. Lightening crackled in a darkened sky. Waves rose up and our ships lurched from side to side. My stomach protested its ill treatment. Most of the lads, who had never learned to swim, were just beginning to make peace with their Maker, when wind blew the clouds away and calm resumed. More than three weeks after our journey had begun, we arrived at the westerly end of the lake called Ontario.

Where we disembarked another river met the lake. We were told the river gave its name to the area as well. This was Niagara. We marched from the docks, past Newark, a town at least the size of Kingston, to our new home: Fort George. Fort George was part of the frontier. It consisted of several wooden blockhouses with second stories projecting out over the first. They were connected by log palisades, enclosing a large parade ground, barracks, officers' quarters, stone powder magazine, kitchens, ovens, a bakery, and a hospital. Huge earthwork redoubts beyond the walls prevented cannon balls from smashing the lower sections of fencing and easy approach. Cannon faced across the river toward an American fort looking back. I hoped that the army had need of us here.

As we settled in we chatted with the men already stationed there. America lay a mere three hundred yards across the river. Their fort was Fort Niagara, a remnant from the French and Indian Wars. It was a stone stronghouse, surrounded by extensive earthworks and wooden stockade, much like Fort George, only positioned better to command the river with cannon. Below its walls, next to the river, was a bustling area known to locals as The Bottom. The Bottom consisted of crude taverns selling cheap whiskey and brothels making other services available. No need for speculation on the origin of the name. We were told that our officers would insist that we resist any temptation to make acquaintance with our American neighbours.

Three days later, Lieutenant-Colonel Sheaffe had us assembled on the parade ground. As Colonel Brock had not accompanied us to Niagara, Sheaffe was in command. We were there to witness a flogging. A soldier, O'Brien by name, was stripped to the waist, tied spread-eagle to a frame, awaiting his punishment. His back glistened with sweat. His body sagged against the frame. Word spread that he had taken a small boat, gone off to The Bottom, and returned drunk, unfit for duty. The price for his misbehaviour was to be high.

Sheaffe, with his officers arrayed behind him, addressed the regiment. "Discipline is necessary in the army. Our frontier circumstance does not alter that fact. We must always be on guard, ready to confront our enemies. Failure to perform our duties and reluctance to obey orders are signs of weakness and poor character. These will betray us in battle. No regiment of mine will betray His Majesty, itself, or me." He paused for effect, then continued. "Using the punishments available to me I will ensure that your behaviour is beyond reproach. I take my responsibilities most seriously. Let there be no mistaking my intentions."

Turning to one of his officers he said, "Proceed with the penalty, Lieutenant. Five hundred lashes."

The young lieutenant, the one familiar with the location of the Canadas, had the ten company drummer boys lined up, jackets and hats removed, ready to administer the punishment. He nodded to the first, who stepped forward, dipped an instrument, nine knotted cords affixed to a wooden handle, in brine and delivered twenty-five blows to O'Brien's back. When finished, the first relinquished the cat-o'-nine tails to the second and moved to the end of the line for the second round. And so it went. Initially, O'Brien struggled to show that he was capable of withstanding the blows, but as the singular welts on his back disappeared into a bloody mass, his body jerked with each blow. By one hundred, blood dripped to the ground. By two hundred, one groan followed another. Somewhere before three hundred he lost consciousness. The young lieutenant who seemed to relish his task ordered the drummer to halt when he observed this, and summoned the surgeon. Examining O'Brien, this officer confirmed with a nod to Sheaffe, he had simply passed out.

Sheaffe again stepped forward. "Let the punishment be halted temporarily. When this man's back has healed we will continue until the full sentence has been exacted." No one thought that he would forget.

Two drummer boys cut the soldier's restraints, and with each one positioning himself under an arm, dragged O'Brien off to the surgery.

I thought Sheaffe's punishment harsh. Five hundred lashes were usually given for desertion. During the flogging I had glanced at the lads about me. I knew I was not alone in my thoughts. Clearly discipline is necessary. Sergeants knew that better than most. But five hundred lashes was more cruel than instructive. We were not at war. No war seemed imminent. American traders moved freely about Fort George by day selling cattle and flour to the British army. I feared that the only enemy we might need to be prepared for was the one in scarlet jacket and gold braid in front of us.

Sheaffe was a man of his word. Throughout the summer he scoured the camp searching for slovenly appearance, improper language, perceived insolence, slackness, der-eliction of duty, and whatever else he thought inappropriate. Stern words, demotion, extra duty, days in the stockade, or flogging would follow. Only sentry duty offered escape from the intense scrutiny of life within the fort.

With my promotion to Sergeant-Major, I had additional duties. I was responsible for setting piquets and searching for deserters absent from their posts. This enabled me to escape to the countryside myself. Colonel Brock had ordered a sentry system for two sections of the thirty-one mile long Niagara River. Fort George provided soldiers for the first section between Fort George and the village of Queenston, seven miles along, where schooners unloaded their cargoes for the portage by ox cart up the escarpment and around the Falls, which I had never seen but heard much about. Fort Erie provided soldiers for the section between Chippawa, with its docks for reloading, and the fort positioned where the Niagara River began. No one could cross the river near the Falls. Men were stationed about a half-mile apart at piles of wood and brush that could easily be set alight in warning. My task was to position them and change the guard daily. Each day I would march men out to replace the ones set there the day before. Officers customarily assigned twenty-four hours of duty, followed by forty-eight hours of rest. How daft an idea was that! Unsupervised, men had difficulty staying awake. There was no urgency or peril to keep them alert. Not infrequently I would come upon a lad asleep at his post. I'd kick his foot to startle the man, rant on about how he'd be dead if an enemy had come upon him rather than me, and threaten to report him to Sheaffe if it happened again. Usually this warning was sufficient.

Sometimes my sentry could not be found. Desertion continued to be a problem. My task was to try and catch the man before he crossed the river. Successful or not, I'd have to report it to Sheaffe.

One afternoon, after the latest desertion, I was readying myself to meet Sheaffe by  polishing my boots and brushing the river road dust from my uniform when two soldiers entered the barracks. O'Brien positioned himself by the door to prevent anyone from entering. Rock, a disgruntled man at the best of times, recently demoted from sergeant for insolence, approached. He sat on the bunk opposite me, glancing furtively about as though someone might unexpectedly materialize. "Things can't go on like this much longer, FitzGibbon."

"What things?"

"Don't play the 'ejit'. You know well enough what I mean. The way his lordship treats us. We'll all feel the lash sooner or later." He nodded in O'Brien's direction.

"What are you proposin' to do about it?"

Rock rubbed his chin as though deciding if he should take me into his confidence, but I knew this was why he had come. "Put officers in charge who know what they're doing."

"Surely you don't think officers will go against their commander. This plan has no chance of success."

"There is great resentment among the men."

"True enough, but no mutiny will succeed."

"We intend to do something, not just sit about polishing our boots. If we do not succeed we'll flee to the United States. We've nothing to lose."

"You haven't left Ireland and come half-way across the world only to be arrested by the King's men here. Come to your senses, man. The situation will be remedied. Some opportunity to improve things will present itself. Stop your foolish thinking."

"You'll not be joining us then, Sergeant-Major?"

"No, I will not. Mutiny is a dangerous proposition. Stay away from me. Have no words with my lads. I want no harm to come to them. Reconsider."

Rock was not seeking advice. He rose and nodded to O'Brien, who turned to face me. He stared long and hard, calculating his next move. I slid my hand to the handle of my sword laid out on the bed.

"If you are not with us, are you against us? What will you do now?"

"I'm thinking that this is just idle talk. Too much drink perhaps. Nothing serious. No intent. That's what I'll say when you're caught if you try to involve me. And caught you will be if you'd don't stop your plotting. Rumours spread. If you persist and your scheming comes to my attention, I'll arrest you and your friend myself."

Rock stomped from the room taking O'Brien with him.

Afterwards, when I found Sheaffe, he was at his desk in the Officers' Quarters, examining some paper. I entered, stopped in front of the desk, came to attention, saluted, removed my cap, and waited. He ignored the distraction of my presence, finished reading, signed and sealed the document. Only then did he look up. "Do you have something to report, Sergeant- Major?"

"Yes, Sir. Another deserter. Private Clarke was not at his post when we went to relieve him."

"Did you attempt to find him?"

"Yes, Sir. I tracked him to Queenston. A small boat was stolen during the night. I borrowed a canoe, crossed the river, and was about to land near Lewiston on the American side where the boat had been abandoned, when New York militiamen stopped me. They delight in desertions and were giving Clarke refuge. They made it quite clear that no access to the United States would be permitted to the British army for the purpose of retrieving recent immigrants. I could do no more."

Sheaffe picked some infinitesimal piece of lint from his jacket, and disappeared in thought. Was he deciding if blame could be attributed to me?

Finally he said, "Desertion must be stopped, FitzGibbon. If flogging doesn't stop this disgusting situation, executing a few men may be necessary to make the point. But of course I can only execute deserters if you do a better job of catching them. Isn't that right, Sergeant- Major?"

"Yes, Sir."

"You'll do better in future I trust".

What was the man thinking! Greater punishments did not inspire greater loyalty. Desertions would increase not lessen. Ruthlessness would agitate Rock and O'Brien. More men would be drawn into their plotting and suffer in the inevitable purge when Sheaffe found out. Should I tell him what I thought? Would Sheaffe listen to reason?

"Is there anything else, FitzGibbon?"

"No, Sir."

He placed the document on his desk into a fine leather pouch and handed it to me. "Take this dispatch to Colonel Brock. Leave on the schooner preparing to depart for York."

I saluted and did as instructed.

Eventually I found Colonel Brock cheerfully overseeing some repair to the York fortifications. Hearing my approach, he looked up from some plan he was reviewing and smiled in recognition. "Sergeant-Major FitzGibbon."

"Sorry to interrupt you, Sir. I bring a dispatch from Lieutenant-Colonel Sheaffe."

"Thank you" he said, yet gave no sign that he intended to reach out and take it from me. "Leave it in my quarters. Will the report say that desertions have diminished?"

"I don't know what it will say, Colonel."

Still smiling, never taking his eyes from mine, he continued. "Fair enough. In your view Sergeant, have the desertions lessened?"

"No Sir, I fear they are increasing. Stories swirl in camp. Farm labourers in America are said to earn three times as much as a soldier. Land is said to be available in the Indiana Territory. It is easy enough for men to cross the Niagara by night to find out for themselves."

"Do you have any thoughts on how to remedy this situation?"

"'Tis not my place to say."

"I am asking for your opinion. I will consider it, as I do the views of others." He turned his gaze from me toward the shimmering lake, perhaps to put me at ease, and waited.

Foolish would it be to speak ill of a senior officer like Sheaffe, but I needed to say something for the sake of the regiment. I hesitated before speaking. "Are you familiar with the fable of the sun and wind, Sir?"

He returned his gaze, blue eyes sparkling, clearly amused at the direction our conversation was taking. "Refresh my memory."

"Yes, Sir. Once upon a time the sun and the wind argued over who was the most powerful. To settle the matter they agreed that whichever one could make the man walking beneath them remove his coat was the strongest. The wind went first. The more he blew, the colder his breath, the more tightly the man gripped his coat to keep it from being blown off. Then came the sun's turn. The sun shone its rays directly on the man. The man warmed and he removed his coat."

Brock laughed. "Do you have any other lesson for me, FitzGibbon?"

"Yes, Sir. I suspect that if the wind continued, the biting cold would cause the man to turn his back and scurry off in the other direction."

"That's rather cryptic."

I didn't know the meaning of the word, but I could guess. I said nothing.

Then Brock said, "Perhaps it's time for me to see Fort George for myself."

Within days I boarded the first schooner bound for Fort George. Apparently Colonel Brock did as well. The day was glorious; remarkably warm for autumn. Sails flapped in the languid lake breezes. Clouds of dazzling white shuffled across the sky. Sunlight sparkled on the water. On shore in the distance, trees blazed in crimson, orange, and gold. The blue of the sky and water wrapped around the ship. Leaning against some cargo on deck, I enjoyed the calm beauty of the day. For a man not fond of sailing, I was spending considerable time on ships.

About mid-day Brock appeared on deck with a book in hand. After standing at the rail for a few minutes surveying the sailors going about their chores, he noticed me. I rose as he approached, but before I could come to attention he gave the order, "At ease." He looked at the book I had in my hand and asked, "A book worth reading, Sergeant-Major?"

"Yes Sir, it's a manual on skirmishing—hiding behind trees and the like. Thought knowing this might be useful in Upper Canada."

"I don't often see off-duty soldiers reading manuals."

"I like to learn as much as I'm able. Is that an interesting book you're reading?"

"It's Shakespeare's Henry V, the story of an English king who triumphs over the French at the battle of Agincourt. I'll loan it to you when I'm finished if you like."

"Thank you. Is there any news of Europe?"

"None good. The peace treaty with the French has failed and we'll be at war with Napoleon soon enough. Do you always ask this many questions, FitzGibbon?"

"There are no answers without questions. May I ask you one more Sir? The men in the barracks have been wagering that a story is not true. I've bet a month's wages that it is."

"I wouldn't want the men in the barracks left wondering. Go on, ask your question."

"It is said that when the regiment was stationed in the Bahamas, you stopped a duelist from killing fellow officers. You accepted his challenge on one condition: that firing be not from twelve paces, but from only one pace away, each of you holding the end of your handkerchief. He refused your condition and left in disgrace. Is this true?"

"True enough. I gambled that he was a coward. You win your bet."

"I was sure I would."

Brock paused for quite a thoughtful moment. "Are you capable of taking correspondence FitzGibbon?"

"I am, Sir."

"I will be needing an aide to assist me. Would this be of interest?"

"Very much."

"Leave it with me." He left me wondering if he meant it, astonished at my good fortune.

When the ship docked outside Newark, Brock left immediately. I stayed behind to help unload some supplies. Upon reaching the fort I was surprised to find the regiment assembled on the parade ground to observe another lashing. A soldier from my company, Hennessy, was strapped to the frame, trying to control his trembling. The air was thick with anticipation. All eyes were on the Officers' Quarters. For ten minutes nothing happened. The silence was louder than most commotions I'd heard. Even birds seemed to stop their chattering. Finally, Sheaffe exited with Colonel Brock trailing behind. The men already at attention stiffened their stance. Sheaffe's angular, humourless face had reddened; he appeared livid. Sheaffe instructed the officer in charge of the flogging, "Let the punishment begin. Twenty-five lashes. Then untie the man." I had not realized that I'd been holding my breath until I heard myself and the others about me exhale.

As the punishment ended, Brock stepped from behind Sheaffe. "Men of the 49th, you have much to be proud of. Even His Majesty knows of this regiment's fine reputation. We do not know when we may be recalled to Europe, or if indeed we will be needed to defend the Canadas. Undisciplined soldiers endanger us all. I promise fair treatment, but orders must be obeyed. Desertion and rebellion cannot be tolerated. These actions will lead to arrest and imprisonment. We must all strive to be the finest soldiers in the British army." A cheer spontaneously erupted. The men had always thought highly of their commander.

Thereafter things were different at Fort George. The intense scrutiny and control of camp life disappeared. Brock permitted off-duty soldiers to fish in the river, shoot fowl for dinner as long as they paid for their powder and shot, and visit Newark if they were properly attired in uniform. Minor infractions were punished with time in the stockade rather than lashing. The men became happier, discipline improved, and desertion stopped.

Unfortunately for Rock and O'Brien and two fellow conspirators, their talk of mutiny had intensified in my absence, and as I expected, came to the attention of officers. These four were transported back to the prison at Quebec. Two months later word was received that a Court Martial had ordered their execution by firing squad.

For me, the year ended with magnificent result. I was promoted to Lieutenant and appointed Adjutant for Colonel Isaac Brock, Military Commander of Upper Canada.

# 5

## *Fort York, 1804*

Not everyone received the news of my promotion with magnanimity. The young lieutenant, for one, felt the need to share his view before I departed Fort George. "Choosing you as his aide is ill-considered. I thought Colonel Brock would show better judgement." The promotion of a sergeant, a non-commissioned officer, to lieutenant was rare. Sometimes in battle campaigns it happened when officer casualties were heavy, almost never in peacetime. Commissions, when available, were usually purchased by men with experience who could afford them. My situation was irregular, but I had no regard for the young lieutenant's opinion. Besides, his scowl told me all I needed to know about whom he thought would be more suitable.

Being an officer provided me with new opportunities for experience. Financially, it proved a mixed blessing. When told of my new pay, I thought I'd inherited a small fortune. One hundred and ten pounds a year was twice what I'd received as a sergeant, six times what a private was paid. Even when my fellow lieutenants joked that I was now as prosperous as a clergyman or small farmer in Upper Canada and would soon earn as much as a shopkeeper if I received further promotion, my mood was not altered. It was only when I learned of my additional expenses that my spirit was dampened. Colonel Brock had waived the purchase of the commission, but I was still expected to dress and act like an officer.

Twenty percent was deducted for meals in the officers' mess and there were uniform items to be secured: a better scarlet coat than the one I had, white cotton breeches for dress occasions, quality leather boots, and an officer's sword and scabbard. No small expense there. And then there was the horse. Officers of the line marched everywhere with their men, but I was expected to accompany the Colonel as he travelled about the province. I required a horse and a saddle, bridle, leather pistol holders—not to mention pistols. And a horse had to eat; fodder was not cheap. Knowing that I had no family to cover these expenses, the Colonel arranged for me to borrow the funds necessary. And so I did, beginning the years and years of debt.

Brock was responsible for the defence of Upper Canada, the thousand miles of frontier borderlands between Lower Canada and Michilimackinac, where Lakes Huron and Michigan meet. As his adjutant, my role was to assist him in his duties by draughting correspondence, carrying his orders and observing their execution, and being his eyes and ears. These tasks were not easy as he was tireless in his efforts to assess and remedy the situation. With instruction I would send out dispatches requesting information, assemble it when returned, assist with reports, and send them off to whomever could authorize expense for whatever improvements the Colonel recommended. It did not take long for us to realize that Upper Canada was ill prepared for any invasion involving more than a hundred ruffians. The dockyards at Kingston required expansion. There were insufficient ships and bateaux for transporting men or provisions. Local farmers could not supply sufficient quantities of food for the army or its Indian allies. There were too few soldiers. The fortifications at York, Niagara, Erie, and Amherstberg at the western end of Lake

Erie all required work. There weren't enough arms, munitions, uniforms, or winter great coats. The alliance with the Indians was fragile. Little was known about the resolve of the people in Upper Canada or the capabilities of the militias. As his eyes and ears I was able to shed some light on these latter two matters.

On one occasion I journeyed into the countryside to secure a horse. The Colonel had provided me with the name of a farmer having some for sale. The army had done business with him before. He was thought to be trustworthy and was willing to accept army bills in payment. Never having owned such an animal before, I sought advice before leaving from an amiable officer known for his horsemanship.

"Surely you've seen a horse before, Fitz. Buy one meant for riding. What else do you need to know?" Of course he was grinning when he said this. When I said nothing and continued to stare at him he responded more seriously. "Two things to remember then. Don't buy one that's too young. You're not experienced enough as a rider to handle one that's not fully trained. And find one with a calm temperament. You don't want one that's easily spooked by the noise or commotion of battle." Armed with this advice and directions to the Woodgate farm, on a horse borrowed from the Colonel, I set off in late Spring to make my purchase.

The farm edged a muddy country road. 'Snake fencing', so called because of the zig-zag placement of the logs, marked its boundaries. Inside the fencing was a band of young apple trees just coming into blossom, with clumps of raspberry cane spaced intermittently. Further back were half a dozen sheep, with mare and foal nearby, grazing in a grassy area. Turning up the lane to the homestead, blue jays scolded me from grand trees for interrupting their day and warned one another of my approach. Sunlight glinted off the shiny buttons on my uniform and the metal plate on the front of my shako that indicated my regiment. To my left, some grain, wheat, or oats,

I could not tell which, was sprouting. To my right, perhaps fifty yards off, a young man was guiding a pair of oxen as they ploughed damp earth, readying it for planting. Ahead, buildings were soon visible: a log cabin with framing for some extension just begun, and a barn of cut timber, two stories high. The cabin was positioned to take full advantage of the shade from a gigantic oak. A briskly flowing creek had been diverted to create a large pond. Blackbirds with red and yellow flashes on their wings trilled from the bulrushes. In the yard there was much activity. A girl placed freshly washed clothing on bushes to dry. A boy of about the same age was leading a cow to pasture. A younger girl fed a flock of chickens not far from an overseeing rooster. Three geese honked their displeasure at a small child who toddled after them. Country smells drifted from the pile of manure near the pigpen. In a paddock next to the barn, a horse ambled about, while another stood at the rail fence observing. A man in well-used clothing, of about forty years of age, lean and muscled with skin creased by the sun, looked up upon hearing my approach. He stopped chopping wood, removed his straw hat, wiped his brow with some old handkerchief, and came forward to greet me.

"Mr. Woodgate? I'm James FitzGibbon of Fort York. I understand you have horses for sale?"

With warm welcome so typical of the inhabitants of Upper Canada, he reached up and shook my hand. "Call me Jacob."

"Fitz," said I, dismounting. "What a gorgeous farm you have, Jacob. There are few farms in Ireland to compare with this. How long since you've settled here?"

"More than a decade now. Our labours are just beginning to show. We've no regrets about coming."

"Where did you come from, if you don't mind my asking? Not from England?"

"No. From Pennsylvania. My brothers are still there. Not farm enough for us all. Since the Revolution the price of land in the territories has been rising. When I heard stories of free land in Upper Canada I came to find out for myself. The government's offer of two hundred acres, seed, tools, and rations for two years was too generous to ignore."

"You're a loyalist."

"Some of my neighbours are. Chased from America after the Revolution they were. That's not a word I'd used to describe myself."

"A patriot, then?"

"No. To receive the land I had to swear allegiance to the King. I'm a man of my word. But I've little concern for whose flag flies in York. Politics won't get a row ploughed or feed my family."

"Easy enough to understand. Are those horses in the paddock available?"

"They are." We moved to get a better look at the frisky chestnut and the watchful brown with a white star on his forehead. "Both are in good health. My eldest son has trained them. He's away now helping a neighbour with a barn that needs building, or I'd get him to show them to you himself. Both can be ridden. The chestnut is two years old; the brown five."

Borrowing equipment from Jacob, I saddled each in turn. I checked their hooves. I clapped my hands unexpectedly to gauge their reaction. The chestnut was the more striking of the two, but the brown was calmer, more steady in his response. "Do they have names? What is the brown called?"

"Guard. Short for Guardian."

"And the chestnut?"

"His name is George."

"In honour of the King or Washington?"

Jacob just winked at me, and said nothing. I must confess that the names influenced my choice. We agreed upon a price for the brown.

Upon completion of our business, Jacob invited me to eat mid-day meal with him and his family. Gathering at a rough-hewn table in the yard we sat, joined by his wife, heavy with child, prayed, and then devoured warm bread, raspberry jam, fresh milk, and apple pie. It was the best I had eaten in a long time.

Returning to the garrison with a pang of homesickness, I described this most marvellous day to the Colonel. He said he envied me my lunch and lamented the lack of affection for our cause held by good men like Jacob Woodgate.

On another occasion I was sent to inspect a militia company whose captain hoped to impress the Colonel. Every male inhabitant of Upper Canada between the ages of sixteen and sixty capable of bearing arms was required to enrol in a militia unit in service of the King. Depending upon the zeal of the militia officers, the unit met regularly or seldom. At a minimum training must take place once a year on June 4th, the birthday of George III. The unit I was to review met in a village on the coach road that skirted the lake to Niagara. As I approached I could see four buildings: a livery stable where horses could be rested or changed, a general store selling whatever might be needed, a tavern, perhaps with rooms for travellers above, and a mill powered by a small river at the far end. In the roadway in front of the tavern small groups of men, farmers of various size, shape, and age, some with musket, some not, milled about. Their mood appeared relaxed and jovial. Rather than ride directly into their midst, I chose to take Guard to the stable for feed and water before going in search of the militia captain. While inside I was able to hear three militiamen conversing beyond the open door. The voices were easily distinguished; The tone of the first was earnest, the second was light and far from serious, the third had a gruff, gravelly quality.

"Don't know why we're doing this. There will never be a war."

"I don't mind a little marchin' and drillin' on a Saturday afternoon. It's a little time away from the missus with a friendly drink afterwards, but gettin' shot at is a different matter."

"Can't be away from home during planting or harvesting," said the earnest one.

"A small little war might boost the price of our crops we sell. Besides, it doesn't matter which form of government we have. Never hear from politicians 'cept when they want something. Better off with no government at all," said the gruff voice.

"Where's the musket the captain gave you?" enquired the first voice.

"Stolen. I'll need another," replied the second voice with no sound of remorse or regret.

The gruff voice chimed in, "Heard you sold it. Better hope the captain doesn't hear that too." After that they passed out of hearing.

I found the militia captain. In his merchant's clothes, top hat, bright red sash, and sword he was easy to see. As I suspected he owned the four buildings in the village. Following some brief conversation and my explanation that I was there on behalf of Colonel Brock, he called his men to attention, perhaps sixty of them. I reviewed the lines of militiamen in their non-existent uniforms, checking to see that the few with guns were holding them properly. Then I joined the captain on the tavern porch to watch as he proudly issued orders to men who performed the drills with little precision or enthusiasm. I nodded with encouragement, careful to mask my true feelings. There was no resolve at all in these Saturday afternoon soldiers.

When I reported these events to Brock he made no attempt to conceal his disappointment.

# 6
## *Fort York, 1805*

As my adjutancy continued into its second year, I came to know Isaac Brock better. One situation in particular revealed his character. A report had come to him that not far from York a bateau laden with musket cartridges, bound for Amherstberg and the western Indians, had run aground. "Fitz," he said, "I've a task for you. Rescue the boat." So off I went with two soldiers from the 49th, Hennessy and O'Byrne, the latter being the lad I'd found asleep on picket duty near Queenston, and ten of the sturdiest men from the Grenadier Company of the 8th Regiment.

The bateau was easy enough to find. There in a foot of water about twenty-five yards from shore, where a river entered Lake Ontario, was the crippled boat. The lake is quite deep, with banks that fall away suddenly, but the river had deposited so much mud and silt that the pilot must have been taken by surprise. My choices were restricted by the need to keep the cartridge powder dry. The wooden cases were too heavy to lift to shore to lessen the load. Even if we'd brought our haversacks, emptying the boxes and bringing the cartridges one sack at a time would take forever. The course of action I favoured was simply pulling the boat from where it was stuck. Stripped down to our grey breeches, we attached our ropes and pulled. Despite our exertions, no matter how much we groaned or complained, it would not be moved. Exhausted, wet, and dispirited, we returned to garrison, unsuccessful. With excuses readied, I reported to the Colonel. "It can't be moved, Sir. It's impossible. We'll need to wait for the autumn rains to free it."

Brock, who had been reading some correspondence, looked up and in a composed, matter-of-fact tone said, "Nothing is impossible." Then he returned to his letter leaving me standing where I was.

The next morning I reassembled my group. "Hennessy, we'll need a waggon and a double team of horses from the stables. There's a sleigh we'll need as well. Load it on the waggon. O'Byrne, see the engineer repairing the south ramparts. Tell him we need to borrow a half dozen of his logs. The grenadiers can help lift them onto Hennessy's waggon. Be ready to leave in an hour."

O'Byrne, anticipating difficulties, asked, "What if the engineer won't release them?"

"Inform him that Colonel Brock has ordered it, and we'll have the logs back before nightfall."

When we reached the immovable object, we used the sleigh to move the heavy cases to shore. The sleigh runners moved smoothly through the mud. Using the horses to raise up the empty bateau, the grenadiers were able to place the logs underneath to reduce resistance. Then with horses and men pulling together we were able to drag the boat to the freedom of deeper water. The task was long and tedious, but by day's end we had returned the bateau to York so it could begin its journey anew.

Before I could enter my quarters I encountered Brock on his way to officers' mess and dinner.

"How went your day, Fitz?"

"Very well, Sir. The bateau will leave for Amherstberg in the morning."

"Well done. My confidence in you was not misplaced. You can tell me more over our meal." And off he went.

In the autumn the Colonel was granted leave to return to his home in Guernsey. Not since they had nursed him back to health from yellow fever, the black vomit as he called it after contracting it in the Caribbean years earlier, had he seen his family. Intending to use his time profitably, I knew that he had other plans as well. He often expressed frustration with the delays in correspondence between the Canadas and London. Replies to requests took months. He planned to take his proposals directly to the Duke of York. One was for a Royal Veterans' Battalion recruited from older retired soldiers in England who might be tempted to Canada should their duties be less onerous; a second was for a light fencible regiment from the newly settled Scots of Glengarry County in Upper Canada; and a third was for voltigeur regiment from the French-Canadians of Lower Canada. Brock could be quite persuasive in person. I suspected he might use this opportunity to petition the Duke for a more active posting in the Napoleonic wars of Europe.

During his absence I was assigned new duties in Montreal and left wondering if I would ever see Brock again.

# 7

## *Quebec, 1807*

The threat of war took us to the citadel to see the Governor-General of the Canadas, Sir James Craig. Isaac Brock was the coveted dinner guest of Quebec society and was familiar with Sir James, but as my dinner invitations usually went astray, I was unacquainted with him. When Brock and I were admitted to his office, Craig, dressed in full uniform, was studying a large map hanging upon a panelled wall. The room itself was all wood and ancient stone. Grey light entered through a pair of casement windows in the exterior wall, effecting a sombre tone. Between the windows was a painting—some red-coated battle scene, memorializing sacrifice and victory; Wolfe dying at Quebec, at a guess. Beneath was Craig's desk. To the side a crackling fire added some warmth and light. Comfortable chairs were companionably positioned in front of the fire. With purposeful strides and a copy of the day's *Quebec Gazette*, the Colonel approached Craig. I hung back by the door so my presence would go unremarked, but I'd still be close enough to hear.

The Governor-General was perhaps sixty years of age, corpulent, and below middle stature. When he turned to greet Brock his movement suggested that he was suffering from some misery.

"Sir James, have you seen the *Gazette?* There are reports that President Jefferson threatens invasion. He professes, and I quote, the acquisition of Canada as far as the neighbourhood of Quebec will be a mere matter of marching."

"Politicians do like to make speeches, don't they? Come Isaac, let's sit by the fire." Uncomfortably, Craig moved toward a cord of fabric on the wall and pulled it before joining Brock in the chairs. "His Majesty's Ship *Leopard* stopped the American frigate *Chesapeake* on the high seas. The Royal navy attempted to retrieve deserters. *Chesapeake* resisted. Damage was done before four men could be collected. This has caused quite a commotion in Washington. The Americans seem incapable of appreciating our predicament. Our navy is all that keeps Napoleon from Britain. If thousands of sailors are permitted to abandon their responsibilities for better pros-pects on American merchant ships, our country's safety will be jeopardized. We must do whatever we must do to remedy the situation."

Brock nodded in agreement. "Their War of Independence was not that long ago. Fresh grievances easily join old ones."

"Washington is in ill-temper at the best of times. The French are confiscating the ships of any nation, including America, that does business both in Britain and on the Continent. Napoleon is forcing nations to choose with whom they trade. Our blockade of the Continent, hoping to cause our enemy deprivations, prevents the Americans from selling or buying goods in France. This leaves the Americans little commerce at all. Their merchants are howling; the financial classes are facing ruin. Jefferson's idiotic policy of retaliation - trying to punish both Britain and France by banning access to the United States of any merchantmen quick enough to elude blockades, only makes their economic situation worse. With no commerce there is little profit, and fewer jobs. Politicians must blame someone. Voters must be appeased."

At that moment a Canadien serving girl appeared and awaited instructions from Sir James. "Deux café, s'il vous plait."

She responded, "Oui, monsieur," curtsied, and left.

Brock referred to the news sheet still in hand. "The war hawks in Congress accuse us of supplying Indians with guns and ammunition and interfering with the westward expansion of the United States."

Sir James grinned mischievously. "Why on earth would they ever think that?" Then continuing more seriously he said, "I do not know if Mr. Jefferson is proposing to take Canada as a prize or to hold it hostage until some concession is granted."

"Do you think there will be an invasion?"

"'Tis difficult to say. Federalist politicians in New England argue for peace and renewed trade with England. Jefferson's Republicans are hard to gauge. Angry speeches are easy to give, but wars are expensive propositions. The Republicans despise paying taxes, on tea or anything else, as much as they hate us."

"I believe we should prepare as though they were serious, Sir James."

"Certainly. It would be foolish not to anticipate that possibility."

"I'll need more soldiers in Upper Canada."

"You may have to do without. Napoleon's defeat of the Austrians at Austerlitz has been followed by a route of the Prussians at Auerstadt and a smashing of the Russians at Friedland. In a blinding snowstorm, of all things! To stop Napoleon, England will need to gain a foothold on the Continent with the greatest army that can be mustered. No troops are likely to be sent here."

"I dearly wish for more active duty. Is there no word on my request for reassignment to Europe, Sir James?"

"No." Craig awkwardly rose from his chair and returned to the map with Brock following. "Where are we most vulnerable in Upper Canada?"

Brock pointed to three separate areas. "Here along the St. Lawrence River, along the Niagara, and at Amherstberg near Detroit."

"Can you not use the militias?"

"I fear if I call out the militias they will not come, and there are too few soldiers to prevent civil disobedience. Should they present themselves when required I worry that the men are not commanded, trained, or disciplined enough to serve my purposes."

The serving girl reappeared carrying a silver tray with matching carafe, sugar bowl, and two porcelain cups. She placed the tray on a side table near the chairs and disappeared. The room filled with a delicious aroma.

"Ah, our coffee," said Sir James. "It's all the rage in Europe. I must admit I've taken quite a fancy to it myself." As Craig poured coffee for himself and the Colonel, he enquired, "And what of our Indian allies? Surely they can be used for good purpose."

"Perhaps," said Brock doubtfully.

"Just remember Isaac, should anyone ask we are only offering comfort and advice to our native friends, not supporting them in their disagreement with the Americans. This is London's official position. No need to antagonize our American neighbours further."

"Yes, Sir."

For some time they gossiped about the latest events in the Quebec social season, then bid one another farewell. As we departed Brock instructed me to make arrangements for a journey to the Six Nations tribes.

# 8
## *Grand River Region, 1808*

"The war chief of the Mohawks is a Scot!" I thought this odd until I remembered the German-speaking English king.

Brock, now a Brigadier General thanks to Sir James, was briefed by William Kerr. He looked very much a government official in his top hat as we were guided to the Indian settlements on the Grand River west of York. "John Norton's mother was a Scot; his father was Cherokee. He was born and educated in Scotland. Came to the Canadas in the British army during the Revolutionary War and stayed . Been a school teacher, fur trader, and interpreter for the Indian Department. Even translated the Gospel of St. John into the Mohawk language. Doesn't always agree with the policies of the Indian Department. Never shy about sharing his views with us."

"A man of some influence then," said Brock.

"Joseph Brant, the great chief who led the Mohawks, the Cayuga, and some of the other Six Nations tribes here at the end of the last war, adopted John Norton as his nephew," replied Kerr.

"You know Norton well?"

"Yes, General. He's a relation. My wife Elizabeth is Joseph Brant's daughter."

The day was warm. Sunshine blessed the fields. There were abundant plantings of corn, squash, beans, peas, and pumpkins—not typical fare in Ireland. Indian women busied themselves with the crops. Men were scarce. I noticed only two as we neared our destination: one returning to the village with fish hanging from a rope, the other heading away carrying both bow and musket as though beginning a hunt. The settlements were confused mixtures of past and present. Bark-covered longhouses capable of holding several families mingled with log cabins and frame houses, not different from those in the mill-centred villages of Dundas and Ancaster that we'd just ridden through.

Kerr led us to a newly-built frame house. On the porch, apparently expecting us, stood a man. The only word to describe him was spectacular. The Indian men we had passed wore deerskin breeches and shirt and beaded moccasins. Their hair was worn in a strip down the middle of an otherwise shaven head. This man was boldly attired. Across his chest, over a brightly patterned, cloth shirt, he wore a red sash—the kind that militia officers fancied. His head was covered with a red scarf, to which a feather from an eagle or large hawk was affixed. Shiny metal discs dangled from his ears. The dominant colour of his clothing suggested where his loyalties lay.

Kerr and I slowed our horses as we approached so that Brock would reach the man first, which he did. "John Norton, I bring you greetings from your King."

"Welcome to the land of the Haudenosaunee," replied Norton, extending his arms wide in a gesture of friendship. "It is an honour to meet at last, the King's warrior I have heard so much about".

We all dismounted, following the General's lead. "As a sign of the King's great affection for you I bring gifts". On cue, as the chief descended the porch stairs, I presented Norton with one of our newest rifles, shined for effect, and an intricately beaded, deerskin cartridge pouch, which he graciously accepted, swinging the strap of the pouch over his head onto his shoulder. He tucked the butt of the rifle under one arm while resting the barrel on the other. "As we speak, waggon loads of food, blankets, muskets, and ammunition are on their way here for your people. Isn't that right Kerr?"

"Yes, General. The supplies will be here for distribution within three days."

"Please accept this as a sign of the King's fondness for all his sons."

"It is good to remind my brothers of the King's concern for them," replied Norton.

"The King has instructed me to make his wishes known to the Haudenosaunee," continued Brock. "Should there be another war with the Americans, he wishes you to join his soldiers in battle."

"I can tell the warriors what you say, but I do not know what they will do. Each man is free to decide for himself. The peace chiefs urge caution. War chiefs like myself urge them to prepare for battle. The warriors listen carefully to all that is said." Norton hadn't lost his accent; I could still hear the intonations of the Scottish highlands.

"Surely, your people must know how little regard the Americans have for Indians. The Haudenosaunee homeland was taken from you only a generation ago. More tribes are being forced from their homes in Ohio, the Indiana Territory, and the Creek lands as we speak, so that land speculators may profit."

"The Haudenosaunee do not forget what has happened. And there are Cherokee, Delaware, and Creek who have found refuge among us because they had nowhere else to go. We have no love for the bluecoats."

"Then why will your warriors not rise up if the King asks them to stand next to his soldiers?"

"Once before," Norton began, "the Haudenosaunee tribes joined the King's soldiers in war. To defend our homeland.

The redcoats fled the field of battle, leaving the bluecoats to do as they wished. They destroyed our crops. Burnt our villages. Tried to starve our women and children. Many of our Seneca, Oneida, Onondaga, and Tuscarora brothers were forced onto reservations in New York. Joseph Brant secured this land for us in payment for our suffering. My people ask if we go to war and the British desert us again, what payment will we receive then?"

Brock assured him, "The King will not abandon his loyal subjects."

Norton stared at the General for a long time before saying, "Promises are easy to give. We will need to see more than hear." Then looking skyward he pointed to some grey clouds in the distance that might hold rain. "The peace chiefs say that if there is to be a great storm, it is best to seek shelter."

In reply Brock gestured to the surrounding settlement. "Do you believe that Haudenosaunee lands will be safe if you hide and do nothing?".

"No. I do not trust the bluecoats. I am a Mohawk. I am not afraid. I will paint my face and be a man. I will not let Yankees chase me from my land. How many warriors will follow me, I do not know." Without realizing it, Norton had cocked his new rifle while he spoke.

"If there is to be a war, I promise it will not be a lost cause. Your bravery will not be wasted," said the General. "Tell me more about your people". Then, sitting on the ground in the Indian style with Norton, he listened to everything the chief had to tell him.

Kerr remained in the Grand River Region to oversee the distribution of supplies that were coming from York, but Brock and I travelled back, intending to spend the night at an inn in the little village of Ancaster, by the waterfall that powered its mill. We rode in silence. Brock seemed to be considering everything that he had learned and the promises he had made. Myself, I hoped the storm would not come too soon. Eventually I asked, "General do you ever wish you were something other than a soldier?"

Without hesitation he replied, "I come from a family of soldiers, Fitz. My father and brothers were soldiers. John died in South Africa. Ferdinand was killed in America at Baton Rouge. You met my brother, Savery, when he was paymaster for the 49th. I cannot conceive of being anything else. I was meant to be a soldier."

"Can Upper Canada be defended, Sir?"

"It can. If I can animate the loyal and control the disaffected. I must inspire confidence in those that live here." Then, as if to amuse himself, he said, "Perhaps all I need do is stand firm, look big, and frighten my enemy away."

Brock laughed as I added, "And that shouldn't be difficult for a gentleman such as yourself."

# 9
## *York, 1810*

*President Madison warns the British: Their Actions may provoke a Second War of Independence.*

*Prices of cotton and tobacco plummet: American economy harmed by British embargo.*

*Congressional 'war hawk' Henry Clay vows to avenge Indian atrocities against white settlers: British will pay for their support of Indian transgressions.*

*Federalist opposition to military sanctions intensifies: bankers refuse to finance war.*

For months, ominous reports from Washington, probably pulled from some American newspaper, appeared in the *Upper Canada Gazette*, frightening the people of York. Information such as this could not be ignored. Apprehension hung in the air like morning mist. Myself, I did not know what to think. American politics was confusing at the best of times. It seemed as though the Federalist politicians who favoured strong centrist government, intimidating armies, and taxes to pay for it all, didn't want a war, while the Republicans in power favoured strong state governments, abhorred taxes, and wanted to proceed as though war with the British Empire would pay for itself. The United States couldn't make up its mind, and until it did, the Canadas would just need to wait and see. It was near impossible to be constantly worried when nothing ever happened, especially when the events described in the *Gazette* had happened weeks, sometimes months, earlier and felt more like ancient history than current events. So when the mid-day sun burnt off the mist, York busied itself with commerce and governmental affairs.

York, often referred to as 'Muddy York' by the locals to distinguish it from 'New York', as though anyone would be daft enough to confuse the two, was proud of its prosperity. For almost two decades it had been the provincial capital and was filled with ambitious men pursuing wealth and influence. Although its population was said to number only seven hundred souls, citizens who considered themselves to be part of 'society' were numerous. There were government officials of all shapes and sizes, and countless merchants who serviced the countryside, exporting or importing whatever was required. Some thought had been given to the layout of the town. Seven streets ran north-south; four ran east-west. Lots, usually fenced, were quite large to accommodate homes, stables, other outbuildings, fruit trees, and gardens, all tended by hired help. The homes themselves were quite substantial. Clapboard covering squared off timber exteriors, brick interiors, and chimneys were all the fashion. Shady elms and oaks had been left during the initial clearing. Fresh water flowed in the many ravines on its way to the lake. The town could boast, in addition to the parliament buildings, one Church of England, a courthouse and jail, a school or two for those who could afford it, a hospital, a library, six hotels for visitors, and nine taverns to keep everyone in good spirits. I was unable to detect any more or less generosity, good will, petty squabbling, envy, or deceit than could be expected in a town of its size. If a person didn't mind the snow and bone- chilling cold of the winter, the muddy streets during spring and fall, or the mosquitoes and dusty, rutted roads of summer, it was a grand place to be.

And of course there was the Lieutenant-Governor's Ball, which was what the purchasers of the *Gazette* really wanted to read about. Once a year the Executive Council, the men who advised the Lieutenant-Government and were responsible for the day-to-day operation of Upper Canada, threw a huge ball in his honour. They invited themselves and everyone else with sufficient social standing so they could show off their daughters. Invitations were customarily extended to all of the British officers at Fort York, so unexpectedly I was permitted to attend.

As the General and I rode from the garrison, past the expanding naval dockyards, to the parliament buildings in the east, I could sense that Brock did not share my enthusiasm for the evening. This was unlike him. "Is there anything wrong, Sir?"

Reluctantly he said, "I received a letter today from my brother, Savery. He tells me that the British army's invasion of the Iberian peninsula has begun. Wellington has landed in Portugal with the intention of moving through Spain to France."

"Surely that is excellent news!"

"And Savery is with them. He has secured a position as an Adjutant."

"Savery is a good man, Sir. He will do himself proud."

"He will, Fitz. I'm happy for him. The thing I'm not happy about is being stuck here, a thousand miles away from an epic campaign, in the same place I've been for eight years, preparing for a war with the Americans that may or may not come. The most exciting thing that happens here is the arrival of my new hat from London."

I understood his frustration. Sometimes I felt that way myself, but thought that this was not the mood to be taking to the social event of the year. "When I was a lad, my Mam always said 'Good things come to he who waits'. That she did. Never seemed like a safe bet then or now."

Despite himself Brock chuckled. "Your Mam said that, did she?"

The ball was being held in the largest building in the town. As we neared parliament, light and music streamed from one of two identical brick structures. Two grey-haired gentlemen smoking cigars stood beneath the covered walkway that connected the buildings, greeting guests as they arrived. My anxiety increased. "General, I've never been to an occasion like this. I don't know any of these people—a few by reputation perhaps, but almost none by sight. I don't wish to offend anyone who thinks he should be known by the likes of me. Will you advise me when it's warranted?"

"Don't worry Fitz, I will. The ball is being held in the Legislative Assembly building. The darkened one is where the Executive Council and the Lieutenant-Governor meet. The two outside are councillors. The one with the mustache is Prideaux Selby. He collects all the revenues for the government. The one with the thinning hair is Judge William Dummer Powell."

Dismounting, Brock said, "Good evening, gentlemen. Exceptionally fine weather we're having."

"A fine evening," replied the Judge.

"Isaac, we were just discussing the imprudence of Judge Wood. Have you heard the story?" inquired Selby.

"No Prideaux, I haven't. What's he done?"

"It was reported to Judge Wood that during the commission of a robbery the thief may have been stabbed in the groin. Wood ordered that all the usual suspects be brought before him. Then he required them to drop their pants. Little evidence was uncovered." Barely able to contain himself, Selby added, " Now everyone is referring to him as the Inspector General of Private Accounts."

"He'll never live that down," replied Brock. "A judge who is subject to ridicule can not be effective."

Powell made no effort to disguise his distaste. " I believe Wood has come to the same conclusion. He's already requested reassignment to Kingston."

Inside stood the guest of honour, flanked by two men equally well dressed. "Sir Francis, I thought I'd find you dancing," said the General.

"Soon enough, Isaac." Glancing to the distinguished older gentleman on his right, then gesturing to the handsome young man on his left, the Lieutenant-Governor said, "You know Aeneas Shaw from our Council meetings, but have you met John Macdonell? I've asked him to join the Council. No doubt he's the finest lawyer in York. We will benefit from his quick, legal mind." I thought he must be a man of promise to gain advancement at such a young age.

"This is my adjutant, James FitzGibbon." Sir Francis and Shaw dipped their heads slightly, acknowledging my presence. Macdonell actually extended his hand to shake mine. Before I could decide if it would be permissible to ask about the health of Sir James Craig, two attractive young women burst into the foyer from the room where violins were being tuned. One led the way while the other tagged behind. Both were attired in high-waist gowns with modestly scooped necks.

"Father, you're monopolizing General Brock. You must release him."

To which Shaw replied, "This insistent young woman is my daughter Sophia. Her companion is Mary Powell, the Judge's daughter."

Addressing Brock directly, she continued. "There are rumours from Quebec that you are an excellent dancer, General."

"I'm sure my prowess is much exaggerated."

"We should judge for ourselves, don't you think?"

"Perhaps you should. May I have the next dance, Miss Shaw?"

"It would be my pleasure." Then, taking Brock on one arm and securing Macdonell with the other, she said, "Come John Macdonell, my friend Mary Powell will do you the honour of dancing with her. How fortunate you are that she is free."

I followed them into the ballroom, positioning myself by the punch table to get the best view. When the music commenced, the men and women arranged in pairs and separate lines began an elegant, moderately paced dance. The more I watched, the more I observed differences between the two young women. Sophia was self-assured and graceful in her movement. She enjoyed the challenge of the dance and had the most bewitching smile. Miss Powell was wary, perhaps fearful she would misstep, noticing which eyes were upon her. She was delicate with a much-admired complexion. Her manner made me think of gentle breezes, rustles, and whispers.

When the music stopped the two couples came for punch, not far from where I stood.

"The stories of your prowess are not exaggerated in the least, General Brock."

"Please, call me Isaac."

"And you must call me Sophia. Our soirées in York must not compare at all with those of London."

"I wouldn't know. I come from Guernsey, an island in the English Channel. I've spent most of my army life in distant lands, and have only been in London once. No soirées were included in my itinerary."

"We must see to it that no opportunity is missed here. A quadrille is beginning. Do not disappoint us, gentlemen. Prove that you fear no dance. Come."

The two couples returned to their places and participated in a lively, intricate dance. I was wondering how and where Brock had become such an accomplished dancer when someone spoke to me. The accent was unmistakable. "An Irishman can't go anywhere these days without running into another one. Are you enjoying yourself, Lieutenant FitzGibbon?"

Next to me stood a man with some greenery jauntily affixed to his lapel. Although his appearance was neat, his fingertips were stained black, perhaps with ink. "You have the advantage, Sir. I must apologize. I do not know your name."

"I'm most disappointed Lieutenant. I imagined that everyone in York knew who I was. You've humbled me. Josephs Willcocks, elected assemblyman, public servant, concerned citizen at your pleasure." He bowed during his own introduction, thoroughly enjoying this pantomime.

"I have heard of you."

"Nothing good, I trust."

'You're the assemblyman who was jailed for contempt by Francis Gore?"

"That I was. The fine gentlemen on the Council don't always appreciate what I have to say about them. They prefer my silence. I challenge their plans. I question how they spend public funds and whom they appoint for government positions. I can't say everything I wish in parliament, but I publish a newspaper in Niagara as well, the *Freeman's Journal.* I can still embarrass and annoy people whenever I want. I'm always looking for stories. I thought you might be a good lad to interview. I promise to refer to you as the gallant James FitzGibbon and use the word dashing at least twice. I'll remind the ladies you're unmarried. You are, aren't you? After I've done singing your praises in print the ladies will be lined up to dance with you. No more standing alone amusing yourself with punch."

"Your interest in finding me lovely companions is appreciated, but my dancing will require great improvement before I'd benefit from such attention."

"I could do a little diggin' and write a story about you whether you'd like it or not. But I won't, for now. If you change your mind, you'll let me know. It'd be a grand story. Is there a war coming, FitzGibbon?"

"We'll all find out in good time."

"So it's like that is it. Just remember FitzGibbon, we live in unsettled times. Opportunities present themselves to men intelligent enough to recognize them. Do you have plans to stay in Upper Canada when your soldiering days are done?"

"Truly, I do not know."

"If you plan to stay, friends are good to have, especially ones with accents the same as yours." Then he turned on his heel and left. Not long after Brock appeared at my side.

"Be careful, Fitz. Willcocks is a very dangerous man."

# 10
## *Fort York, 1811*

After reading the latest dispatch from Quebec, General Brock asked me to assemble, with some urgency, his advisors: Captain John Glegg of the 49th, a taciturn veteran who chose to hide half his face behind a bushy mustache, William Kerr from the Indian Department, and John Macdonell, proudly wearing his new uniform. Macdonald's inclusion in this advisory group was not surprising. Since the Lieutenant-Governor's Ball, he and the General had become the best of friends. On numerous occasions they'd discussed ways of improving militia selection and training. Eventually, the General appointed Macdonald to be Lieutenant-Colonel of the York Militia to take full advantage of his zealousness. Personally, I found John to be an amiable, energetic, and enterprising young man. A little quick with decision-making perhaps, but at least he wasn't challenging fellow lawyers to duels anymore. Fortunately for all concerned, his last challenge had not been accepted.

With the exception of Captain Glegg who preferred to stand, we sat at a table in officers' quarters, waiting for the General to inform of us of the latest developments. The seriousness of the situation was conveyed in his demeanour. "The United States may be guilty of an Act of War. His Majesty's Ship *Guerriere* stopped an American merchant ship in coastal waters to search for deserters from the British navy. Apparently, *USS President* was sent after *Guerriere* to express its disapproval. In fog, *President* mistook unsuspecting *HMS Little Belt* for *Guerriere* and fired upon her. The smaller, outgunned *Little Belt* was blown to pieces. Many British sailors have been killed and wounded. How can this be ignored? In addition, reports emanating from Washington say that the U. S. Congress has approved expenditure necessary to increase the national army from ten thousand to twenty-five thousand soldiers. What is to be made of this? I have been summoned to Quebec. Sir James' ill-health has necessitated his return to England. I will be meeting with his successor, Sir George Provost, (Brock pronounced his name pray-vo in the French fashion). No doubt Sir George will require me to apprise him of the situation here. I do not wish to neglect anything. Glegg, how many British soldiers are stationed in Upper Canada?"

Glegg replied succinctly. "Sixteen hundred regulars spread across seven garrisons."

"That's what I thought. William, is there any change in the disposition of the Six Nations?"

"John Norton continues to have his followers and advocates for our cause, but the Six Nations have made no commitment. However, there are developments further west in the Indiana Territory. Apparently, the Americans find what is happening alarming. The displaced tribes from Ohio are joining the threatened ones in Indiana. Miami, Potawatami, Kickapoo, Ottawa, Huron, Chippewa, and Wyandot are meeting with the Shawnee at a place called Prophetstown on the Tippecanoe River. Two Shawnee brothers talk of an Indian confederacy. The younger brother, the one with the deformed eye, Tenskwatawa– the Prophet, awes them with a mixture of magic and witchcraft, then preaches a return to traditional ways. He demands they abandon alcohol, gambling, quarrelling, and stealing from their brothers. The older brother, Tecumseh, is said to be quite an orator. He urges the tribes to forget past grievances with one another and to form an alliance. He says that now is the time to take a stand against American encroachment on ancestral lands. Sioux, Saulk, and Winnebago from the far west have come to hear him. Indian agents tell me that even now he journeys to Georgia to meet with the chiefs of the great Creek Nation."

"That situation holds promise. Keep me informed, William."

"Yes, Sir."

"John, what about the Militia?"

"There are thirteen thousand men spread across Upper Canada eligible for militia service."

"Doubtful characters most," interrupted Glegg.

Turning to look directly at Glegg, Macdonell continued. "It is true Captain, some can not be relied upon. I grant you that, but remember a third of the province is Loyalist. Either they or their parents were forced to flee the United States fearing for their lives when the British lost the War of Independence. Some men even fought against the Americans, and most knew people who died. Some were beaten, tarred, and feathered by mobs. Most knew people who were imprisoned for their beliefs. All of them had their property confiscated for not supporting the revolutionary cause. Bitterness remains."

"The American revolutionaries were intolerant of dissent. They believe in freedom of speech, but you'd better not disagree with them," commented Brock.

"The Loyalists won't let the Americans take away their property a second time. Then there's people like me who were born in Britain. We can be counted upon," said Macdonell banging his fist upon the table.

"Perhaps the best course of action is to separate the loyal and committed from the uncertain," said Brock, summing up. "Fitz, send a letter from me to every militia commander in the province. Order them to select from each one hundred men available to them the ten or twenty who will make willing and able soldiers. We'll place them in flank companies suited for skirmishing. We'll supply and train them to a high standard and outfit them as best we can. We'll even provide some uniforms if we can find any. The army will reimburse the men for time away from their farms or businesses. Work with John on this while I'm away. The militia officers should be informed that Lieutenant-Colonel Macdonell will be meeting with each of them soon to assess their progress. John, once they've done what I've asked, supply them with the materials needed. Anything else, Fitz?"

"Just one thing, General. Ship construction at Kingston has accelerated. The commodore reports that British and American navies on the lakes are evenly matched. There should be no disruption of our supply lines."

Digesting everything that had been said, Brock thanked us. We rose from our chairs and wished him safe journey.

Two months later I'd ventured to the docks, wondering if the General might return on this latest schooner arriving from Quebec. And there he was, disembarking, with distinctive epaulettes on his new scarlet coat and an attendant leading a magnificent, black stallion.

"Are the markings on your jacket those of a Major-General, Sir?"

"That they are, Fitz. They certainly are. London must have read and appreciated all those fine reports we've sent them. I'm now in command of all military forces in the Canadas, and I'm to replace Sir Francis Gore as the Administrator of Upper Canada."

"And the British army has given you a horse for your troubles? I'll need to pursue advancement more intently if every promotion brings such a horse with it."

"Sir James left him for me. A generous gift."

"There's to be no response from London regarding *Little Belt?*"

"They've chosen to ignore the affront to devote full attention to Napoleon."

When the General stopped to inspect some construction on the fortifications, I questioned him further. "What is your opinion of Sir George?"

"Provost is a cautious, little man. He fancies himself quite the diplomat. He believes in compromise, conciliation, and dinner parties. He thinks that negotiation will win the day, and the Americans can be dissuaded from war. Ladies' perfume from too many soirées must have damaged his senses; he can't recognize the smell of animosity in the air. And if the decision about promotion had been left to him, his old friend Sheaffe would be the new Major- General."

"We'll receive no more regulars then?"

"He doesn't believe it should be necessary. However, in the unlikely event he is mistaken, he has asked me to devise a strategy to protect stronghold Quebec. Five thousand soldiers are to remain at his disposal in Lower Canada. His reputation is paramount. There will be no advancement should he ever lose Quebec. Upper Canada has only his best wishes. Moreover, he requires me to behave scrupulously and avoid any act that might irritate the government or people of the United States."

Before the General could share any more of his thoughts on Sir George, we saw John Macdonell excitedly riding to where we stood. "Welcome back, Isaac. You and Fitz shall be the first to hear my good news. Mary has consented to be my wife. Judge Powell has given his permission. What a glorious day! I'm off to inform my parents."

"She's a fine young woman. Congratulations, John," said the General. I extended my best wishes too before he galloped off. "There goes a happy man, Fitz. The idle hours of the passage from Quebec provided me with ample opportunity to consider my own happiness. I have come to realize how fond I am of Sophia. The sparkle in her eyes brightens my days."

"I'd always taken you for a career officer. Thought you'd be waitin' until your adventure was done before you'd be settlin' down in England with a local lass, or at least the lass whose father owned the splendid manor house next door."

"That's what my eldest sister Elizabeth recommends. In her letters she constantly alerts me to the suitable, young women she meets. They don't need to live next door, as long as the neighbourhood is respectable. She scolds me when I show little interest in her schemes."

"There's nothing to keep you from doing what you want."

"Actually there is, but you must keep this in the strictest confidence, Fitz. Regrettably, I am in no position to take a wife at this moment. My brother William loaned me the funds necessary to purchase my commissions when I first joined the army. His bank has suffered unexpected set-backs. I've pledged my income to him until the difficulties have passed. I have no money myself now, and am not certain when I shall have some. Only time will tell."

# 11
## *York, January 1812*

Stout evergreens sheltered beneath their blanket of snow. Trees that had lost their leaves stood forlornly, with branches reaching into the night sky towards the frozen moon and stars. Frost on the brittle bushes glistened in the moonlight. Nothing moved; even fox and other predators were not about. Silence, like the cold, had descended on everything. The only thing to be heard was the crunch of the snow with each of my footsteps and the sound of my own breathing.

I would not have ventured out on such a winter's eve if it hadn't been for the dispatch. The letter had come all the way from London, I could tell from the wax seal. And some poor bugger had been sent with it from Quebec in the midst of a Canadian winter.

My grey greatcoat, fur cap, and mitts offered little consolation as I trudged along, heading for the home of Aeneas Shaw where I suspected Brock might be. Coming up the path to the house I thought I could see a scarlet coat through the curtainless window of a front room. To be sure I paused on the veranda steps and peered in. Candlelight illuminated the room. The General was seated on a piano bench next to Miss Sophia, who was playing some lively tune. With great affectation he was singin' along. Brock was actually singing!. She was clearly enjoying his rendition. Flames from the fire danced in the hearth. I could imagine the warmth and comfort of that room. When the song was done there was enthusiastic applause. Other family members must have been observing the performance. Another tune began, and this time Miss Sophia mirthfully joined in the duet. For a moment I was filled with longing and deep regret that there was no soothing touch, companionship, or simple joy in my own life. It seemed heartless to disturb them, but I grasped the lion's head knocker in my hand and rapped loudly on the door.

A servant opened it, shivered with the blast of cold wind that accompanied me, and waited for some explanation of my presence, although my uniform and the letter in my hand surely gave it away. "For Major-General Brock."

With the sound of my voice, Brock appeared in the drawing room doorway with Sophia peeking around his shoulder. "Fitz, what brings you out on such a night?"

Extending my hand I said, "My apologies, General, but I feared this might require some urgent response."

Brock broke the seal of the envelope and read the message within. He attempted to reveal nothing in his expression, but the clenching of his jaw concealed little. Turning to Miss Sophia he said, "Forgive me, dear. This matter requires my attention." He kissed her on the cheek and left, leaving his winter coat and hat behind.

With some alarm in her voice she asked, "Fitz, why does Isaac leave so suddenly? What is in that letter?"

"Don't know, Miss. Please excuse me." Grabbing his belongings from the wooden bench in the hall, I went after him.

A short distance away Brock leaned against a stone wall. In the severe cold each breath could be seen when he exhaled. The slow pronounced movement of his chest suggested he was struggling for control. He starred up at the darkened sky.

"Has the invasion begun, Sir?"

"Not yet. Soon enough."

"What's the matter then?"

"A position in Spain on the Duke of Wellington's staff has become available. He has offered it to me. It's to be my decision. It's what I've dreamed of."

I could not comprehend the meaning of his words. If Brock was leaving for Spain there was no hope for the people of Upper Canada. Their lives would change forever. "Will you be leaving, General?"

He starred into the sky for a moment longer, as if the answer might be found there, and then looked directly at me. "No. Duty requires me to stay. I can't abandon this country after spending most of my life preparing to defend it, just as the muskets are raised."

# 12
## *York, May 1812*

Brock was sitting at his desk, fingertips of his two hands pressed together, forefingers touching his lips. When he noticed my presence he launched into the details of his day. "Willcocks is leading the opposition to all of my proposals in the Legislative Assembly. The western tribes are assembling at Amherstberg seeking sanctuary after the destruction of Prophetstown. They need to be fed. Some assemblymen object to this expense. Laws permitting the arrest of citizens suspected of treason need to be passed, but there is resistance to this as well. Willcocks argues that citizens have rights; he says nothing will justify the suspension of rights, even suspicion of treason, if we are not at war."

"I do not understand the opposition, Sir," said I.

"Some of the assemblymen mistakenly believe that war will never come. No unpleasant actions need be taken. Others wish no laws to encumber them until they can feel which way the wind is blowing. If there is to be a war, they may wish to switch sides if it seems in their best interests. Only the Loyalists can be counted upon."

"What will you do?"

"That's just what I was considering when you entered. I think it's time to control the disaffected, beginning with Willcocks."

"He thinks highly of himself, Joseph does."

"Perhaps we can take advantage of that. We need to redirect his energies. Fitz, I have a task for you."

The following afternoon, dressed in civilian clothes, I found myself in the darkened interior of the Wayward Son, one of the many taverns in York, places men frequented when they wished to discuss the events of the day. The bar consisted of freshly-cut boards set on upturned boxes resting on dirt floor. A wooden keg sat on the counter, holding beer likely brewed in the barn out back. Planks behind the bar served as shelves for glass jars used for drinks, and bottles of some lightly coloured, distilled spirit. The room was filled with noise, stale air, and the slightest smell of sawdust emanating from where it had been sprinkled on the floor. The man behind the bar had a ruddy complexion; he looked like someone who enjoyed what he sold and was muscular enough to toss anyone causing a disturbance into the street with little ceremony. The long wall opposite the bar was shuttered so that air or light could be admitted, should any patron want to remember what either felt like. At the far end of the room, furthest from the entrance in front of a brick fireplace which could be lit when cold or night gave no other option, was Joseph Willcocks, regaling listeners with some fanciful story. When I caught his eye, he excused himself from his companions and joined me at my end of the bar.

"Well, well. James FitzGibbon. Are you here to buy me a drink?"

"Perhaps I am," I said signalling the barman for two beer.

"I must admit I hadn't expected to find the likes of you in a disreputable place like this."

"You're not an easy man to find."

"Surely you weren't lookin' in The Crown or The Three Lions. Too many Englishmen for my taste. Have you changed your mind about bein' written up in my newspaper?"

"Not yet. I'm considerin' it. When I'm ready for all the attention of those women readers of yours I'll let you know."

"Why have you come then? Don't tell me you want to join those of us who intend to resist oppression in whatever form it takes, and speak out against laws that restrict a man's right to do as he wishes!"

"I always enjoy a fine speech, but I'm here on the General's behalf."

"Mister High-and-Mighty has a message for me? Why doesn't he just give it me himself?"

"The General doesn't frequent The Wayward Son."

"Do him some good if he did. Meet some of the people he governs, he would."

"Brock doesn't share your politics..."

"He's said so often enough."

"....but he admires persuasive men who stand up for what they believe. He thinks you'd make an excellent emissary for the government."

"An emissary to whom?"

"To the Six Nations. They're wavering. He needs them to commit to the British cause. He thinks you're the man who could make that happen."

"What's the real reason he's not asking me himself?"

"He wants your service, but he won't give you the satisfaction of turning him down. If you choose not to, he'll deny ever asking you. And as far as I'm concerned, this conversation never happened."

"Makes sense. Why would I want to be doin' any favours for the High-and-Mighty?"

"Because you're someone who could make it happen. You've a way with words. You're persuasive. If he thought someone else could do a better job, he'd ask them instead. Should you fail, no one will ever know you were engaged in this endeavour. Should you succeed, Brock promises to recognize your efforts. There's a chance for public acclaim."

Willcocks' eyes bored into me. Sweat from my armpits trickled down my sides. He rubbed his middle fingers across his lips while he calculated what would be in his best interest. Eventually he said, "An interesting proposition, this. I'll consider it."

I pressed on. "General Brock instructed me that I am to leave with an answer, yea or nay. He won't be kept in uncertainty, and he won't make the request a second time." Then I waited.

"Aye," said Willcocks. "I will act as the government's emissary."

"William Kerr will guide you to the Grand River. He'll bring offerings for you to give to the Six Nations. Can you be ready to leave within the week?"

"I can."

"Grand. I'll inform the General. Kerr will contact you with details. This should be an opportunity for you to show the kind of man you are." Then I departed, leaving the intense scrutiny behind.

Brock was elated with my news. "This task will either involve Willcocks and attach him to our cause, or at least preoccupy him for awhile. Well done, Fitz. But you'd better draft a letter to John Norton explaining my purpose in sending Willcocks to him so he'll know what to expect. I don't want him to be offended by anything that man says."

# 13

## *Fort George, June 1812*

The American officers, resplendent in their navy jackets and white breeches, in uniforms not that much different from our own, had just left the dinner at Fort George to cross the river before dark. General Sheaffe had invited them. To Sheaffe we were all comrades-at-arms, professional soldiers. We were gentlemen with one exception, sharing a common bond, and easily capable of enjoying one another's company. Myself I was not entirely comfortable with this explanation for befriending the enemy, but knew enough to keep my mouth shut.

Preparations for dinner had been extensive. The camp wives made more than a few shillings washing and ironing the linen, polishing the silverware, and setting out the fancy plates reserved for special occasions. The glassware sparkled in the candlelight from the chandelier. Sheaffe must have truly wanted to impress the Americans as no expense was spared. The meal itself was delectable: roast fowl, boiled ham, baked fish, and an array of summer vegetables. The wine, better than a poor lieutenant could afford, was magnificent. Glegg, Macdonell, and I had remained at the table with Sheaffe, not wanting the last of the wine to go to waste. We were discussing whether or not Napoleon would be mad enough to invade Russia when General Brock entered the room, letter in hand.

He looked very much the man whose moment had come and would not be found wanting.

"Gentlemen, a week ago the United States Congress declared war on Great Britain. Sympathizers to our cause sent word to Sir George by voyageur as soon as the announcement was made. London still does not know."

No one said a word. The only noise came from Macdonell's chair as he rose, readying himself for action. I glanced quickly at the others. Glegg, more grim-faced than usual, seemed a man just told of some onerous task required of him. Sheaffe's expression was harder to gauge. At a guess, he seemed more like a man estimating how a good war might improve his career prospects. As for myself, a great sadness overcame me. The only thing that came to mind was the suffering that would inevitably come to the Canadas.

Reading from his letter Brock continued, "Sir George has included his instructions to me along with the news: No offensive operations are to be undertaken unless they are solely calculated to strengthen our defensive attitude." He paused before glancing up at us.

"There are less than eighty thousand people in Upper Canada, less than half a million in both Canadas and our maritime colonies combined. The United States has fifteen times that number. Waiting for the American invasion will not work in our favour. We must act quickly, and do damage before Goliath knows what hit him!"

Macdonell spoke. "Isaac, do you think they'll assault Montreal first?"

"They should, to sever our supply line from Quebec, but I don't believe they will. There is diminished support for the endeavour in the New England states, and their army is not yet prepared to advance on our strongholds. Moreover, the taste for war is strongest among those wishing to crush the Indian resistance. I believe the invasion will begin in the west."

Glegg asked simply, "What needs to be done, General?"

"Fitz, send an order to Captain Roberts at Fort Joseph. With the aid of his Indian allies he is to secure Fort Mackinaw before the American garrison knows there even is a war. As for us, we'll leave for Amherstberg as soon as we are able. General Sheaffe, continue preparations for the defence of Niagara while we are gone. The Americans will be here soon enough."

# 14
## *Fort Amherstberg, August 1812*

Fort Amherstberg is situated on the Detroit River where the waters of the upper lakes empty into Lake Erie. When we arrived, Amherstberg was in total disarray.

Lining the road to the sentried gates of the fort were innumerable waggons overflowing with people transporting a sizable portion of their worldly goods. Wooden barrels, sacks of grain, crates of chickens and roosters, and tools of every description were stacked next to prized family possessions. One family even had a small harpsichord stowed beneath bedding. Everyone was waiting to be admitted, but none of that was happening.

Surrounding the fort was a massive encampment. There were hundreds of wigwam, dome-like structures covered with bark and animal skins, enough for thousands of Indians. Women tended cooking fires that sent smoke drifting lazily into the air. Children with bows and arrows chased one another about. Warriors stared watchfully as we passed.

Within the wooden palisades there was even greater crowding and commotion. It was nearly impossible to move. Countless waggons clogged half of the parade grounds. The smell of animal excrement stung the nostrils. Oxen, working horses, cattle and goats were all tethered to the giant wheels, and made enough noise to make me believe that secretly Amherstberg had been transformed into a farm. Groups of men and women with sun-creased faces stood aimlessly about in their straw hats and cloth bonnets having grim conversations with one another while small children skittered about in the shade beneath the waggons. A boy chasing a squealing piglet attemptin' some escape made me smile.

On the other half of the parade grounds, canvas tents were clustered closely together and a company of redcoats was being put through morning drill by a disapproving sergeant who had no difficulty being heard. From the yellow facing on their uniforms I knew they had to be lads from the 41st, another regiment recruited in Ireland. Several dozen Indians, Mohawks with partially shaven heads, stood with John Norton watching this military display. Outside the trading post another group of natives stood with piles of fur and animal skins, hoping to barter for whatever they required Somewhere regimental drummers practised musical commands in case officers' orders couldn't be heard on the battlefield.

As we mounted the steps of the command centre with the Union Jack fluttering above, General Brock said to me, "Fitz, find out why all of these settlers are here. I'll be with Proctor. Join us when you're finished."

So I turned and approached two men standing next to waggons nearby. These were rugged men, accustomed to hard work. I introduced myself and enquired after their circumstance. One of the settlers introduced himself as Jarvis, the other Marintette. Jarvis' wife, distress clear in her eyes, joined us. All three were willing to talk and chimed in without much prompting. Jarvis began. "The American soldiers came to our farm. They took what they wanted—our livestock, the corn we'd just put in the barn, the flour we'd milled, the apple cider we'd pressed, and the jam and preserves the wife had just set aside for winter."

"They ransacked our house," added his wife. "This is all that we have left!" She pointed to a near-empty waggon, holding mostly farm implements, some kitchen furniture, bedding, and enough straw to feed the oxen for a couple of days.

"I could do nothing to stop them. Muskets were levelled at us. I asked, 'What will we eat? You're takin' everything we'll need in winter. How will we warm ourselves? You're stealin' our blankets and the wood we've chopped for our hearth.' Their only reply was that they were hungry, tired of what their army considered food, and cold at night. We were of no concern to them."

"We leave tomorrow," said the wife. "The children and I go to stay with my brother. He has a farm on the Thames River. Thank God he offers us refuge. My husband will stay and fight with the militia."

Then Marintette spoke up, in English with the French-Canadian pronunciation so familiar to me from my days in Montreal and Quebec. "My farm may be next, so I gathered my family and we came here for protection." Quickly surveying the meagre detachment of soldiers on the fort walls and the state of the fort's defences he added, "But these soldiers will have difficulty defending themselves from the army at Detroit."

While Marintette was speaking, Jarvis retrieved a poster from beneath the seat of his waggon and handed it to me. "Lieutenant FitzGibbon, have you seen General Hull's Proclamation? It's nailed to trees along the main roads where everyone is sure to see it. He promises to rescue the inhabitants of Upper Canada from the tyrannies of the British."

"Where is this British tyranny?" asked Marintette. "We live in peace. No one bothers or molests us. Hull is the one who threatens. He says that unless we welcome him with open arms he will treat us as enemies who deserve whatever horrors befall us."

"Hull warns us to choose wisely or he will bring war, slavery, and destruction," added Jarvis.

With rising panic in her voice, his wife asked me, "What will become of our farms? Will the American soldiers keep them as prizes of war?"

Glancing at the Proclamation, one disturbing phrase caught my eye. 'This is to be a war of extermination.'

"Hull warns that no white man fightin' on the side of an Indian will be taken prisoner," said Jarvis. "Instant destruction will be our lot, says he. Does he not know that every man is required to serve in the militia, and all militiamen fight next to Indians? Does he plan to kill us all?"

I had no answers to give to any of their questions, not knowing what the Americans intended to do.

Jarvis continued with great certainty. "The Americans force us to choose sides. T'was not my intention to involve myself in this dispute, but involve me they have. There is only one choice, and it's not to beg for mercy from someone who steals my food and tells me I am of no concern."

I thanked them for their candour and extended my best wishes for their safety. Regrettably there was little else I could do to help. With their permission I took the copy of the Proclamation to the General.

Inside, the General sat in front of the desk that Colonel Henry Proctor sat behind, fingering a silver letter opener as he complained about the difficulties of command. "The Nitchies continue to be a burden. I'm not sure why they're here. Do we need them? Can't they go elsewhere? There isn't enough food. I am told that fourteen head of cattle and seven thousand pounds of flour are procured each day to feed them. My commissary officer informs me that the farmers don't have excess to sell. And some won't accept British army notes in payment. They fear they'll be worthless if we lose the war."

Brock said simply, "Ingenuity is certainly required in such a situation."

Considering Proctor's ample girth and snug-fitting uniform, I doubted that he was going hungry because he shared many meals, or losing sleep worrying about the native condition. This was someone who enjoyed his small indulgences.

"And the Nitchies don't obey orders. My commands are regarded as mere suggestions. They skirmish with the Americans when they wish to. Won't stand and fight like soldiers. Don't trust them."

"We have given them little reason to trust us," said the General. "For fear of antagonizing the Americans, Britain has not always come to their aid. Now our goals are perfectly aligned. What do you know of the army at Detroit?"

This was a matter Proctor was happy to discuss. He stopped fiddling with the letter opener.

"The Governor of the Michigan Territory, General Hull, is an old man, a relic from the Revolutionary War. His incursion across the Detroit River, north of us, was nearly a month ago. He skirmished with the Indians, then retreated."

"Why would he do that?" asked Brock.

"He doesn't know that his army vastly outnumbers ours. I believe he is waiting for reinforcements. We intercepted a schooner, the *Cuyahoga Packet*, carrying Hull's official papers and possessions. The documents reveal the actual strength of his regiments, and his overestimation of ours. At present he has twenty-five hundred men: five hundred regulars from the Fourth Infantry and two thousand militia from Ohio and Kentucky. As well they have at least twice as many cannon as we do. He would be shocked to learn that I have only four hundred redcoats, and God knows how many Upper Canada militia, at my command."

"If he even imagines he has an advantage, why doesn't he attack?"

"His letters reveal that he is terrified of the Indians. His daughter-in-law and his grandchildren are with him. The thought of the scalping knife horrifies him."

"Thank you for your report, Colonel. Send Hull's correspondence to my quarters so I can review it myself. Is Tecumseh at Amherstberg?"

Proctor nodded, as a gentleman might if he had just been asked to confirm there was a mud on his boot.

"Does he speak English?"

"Well enough when he's scolding me, General."

Glegg, Kerr, and I followed Brock as he left Proctor. Outside I enquired of Kerr why Proctor had referred to the Indians as 'Nitchies'.

"The greeting of the Ojibway is 'Slaygo niigii'. It means 'welcome friend'. I don't believe our Colonel shares the sentiment," was his reply.

"Is Hull right to be so afraid of the Indians?"

"For more than half a century, since the French and Indian War, there has been no shortage of cruelty on the frontier. Both Indians and Americans have been guilty of savagery. The killing of Indian women and children has been matched with the killing of white women and children. Scalps of the enemy have been taken as trophies. Kentucky militiamen carry long knives to scalp more easily. Not all behave this way, but there has been too much mutilation and desecration of bodies. Pure hatred can make a man do many things."

Later that afternoon Brock went in search of Tecumseh. We found him on the edge of the Indian encampment under a tree with a group of young men sitting around him, listening to his every word. When Tecumseh saw us he left his group and came forward. In some ways he looked little different from other natives; he was copper in colour, with shoulder-length black hair, deerskin clothing, and moccasins ornamented with porcupine quills. Still, there was something about him. His face was chiselled to reveal determination and defiance. Around his neck he wore a silver medallion stamped with the face of some English king. His eyes dared you to try and take the medallion from him. I'd been a soldier long enough to know that underestimating this man would be a mistake.

Brock glanced at Kerr, who had come along to interpret should Proctor have exaggerated the war chief's comprehension of English. Kerr nodded, confirming that Brock had found the man he wanted. "It is an honour to meet the great Shawnee warrior, Tecumseh, feared war chief of the western tribes."

"It is true. I am Shawnee. My forefathers were warriors. Their son is a warrior. Are you here to help us, Brock?"

"I am."

"My people have been waiting for you to come. The bluecoats want our land. They grow angry when we do not give it to them. Why not ask for the water and the air as well? They offer us liquor and trinkets. They say we should be content with plots of land." Tecumseh nearly spat out the word 'plot'. "Our forefathers were hunters. We are hunters. Will the animals of the forest stay on our plots of land?" With increasing bitterness in his voice he continued. "When we say that we do not wish to sell the land given to our ancestors by the Great Spirit, the bluecoats come to take it from us. I have stood on the ashes of my village, held members of my family while they died in my arms, and buried friends who died defending their homes. Can I walk away? Greed plugs the ears of the white men. They can no longer hear the pleas of my people. Peace with the Longknives is not possible."

"Together, as allies, we can defeat the bluecoats."

"What will happen to us when this is done?"

"The King wishes his native sons to have a homeland. The Michigan Territory and more will be yours."

"We have heard promises before, but they vanish in the wind like the birds of autumn."

"Tecumseh, I speak the truth. When the smoke of our muskets blows from the battlefield you will see the war chief of the redcoats standing next to you. If we are victorious, as long as I have breath, I will remind the King what his native sons have done, and what I have promised here today on his behalf."

"The elders say watch what a man does, then listen to what he says. Word of the capture of Fort Mackinaw has reached us. Will we now go to Detroit?"

"Yes."

Tecumseh unravelled a strip of elm bark and, going down on one knee, placed it on the ground. With his knife he scratched out what appeared to be a map. Brock went down on one knee to look. They conversed for some considerable time and reached agreement. As we walked away, Tecumseh said something in a native tongue loudly enough for his young warriors to hear. I asked Kerr to translate for me. "There is a man," was his translation.

Following the meeting with the chief, the General ordered Proctor to have his regulars from the 41st and the flank companies of the Norfolk, Oxford, and Essex County militias ready to cross the river in two days time. They would be joined by the York militiamen that Macdonell was busily outfitting in the remnants of cast-off redcoat uniforms we had brought with us. Proctor urged the General to reconsider his plan, but he said, "I intend to engage the enemy at my pleasure, not his." Then with Proctor's fine glassware and best bottle of wine coerced from the Colonel's private collection, Brock proposed a toast, "To Valour." Who wouldn't drink to that?

At dusk on the eve of battle, Brock wandered among the army tents commending enlisted soldiers and militiamen alike, reminding them of the importance the next day's action. This gesture was well received. We visited the docks where bateaux were being labouriously loaded with ammunition, an artillery piece, horses, and other supplies. Our inspection was interrupted by beating drums coming from the direction of the Indian encampment. We followed the sound.

Hundreds of warriors were circling a giant bonfire, chanting to the mesmerizing beat of the drums. They moved from one foot to the other in a dance. Stripes of paint marked bare chests and arms. More paint—red, white, and black mostly—covered faces. The colours made me think of blood, life, and death. Flames from the fire flashed red, orange, and yellow. Embers crackled and sent sparks darting into the darkness. Sweat glistened on bodies. Tomahawks and war clubs waved in the air. Although the men moved about, it was if they had gone into a trance. What visions of bravery could they see? Suddenly the drums stopped. Tecumseh appeared from the darkness. In his loudest voice, with arms raised skyward, he spoke in his native tongue. Kerr translated what he said. "Warriors. Our enemies have come to take away the lands given to us by the Great Spirit. We are brave, but they are many. The Great Spirit sends us the strength and courage we need. He has sent the redcoats to help us. Tomorrow only the shout of victory will come from our mouths."

The warriors then burst from their trances, grabbed muskets and cartridge pouches nearby, and dashed to their canoes on the riverbank, whooping loudly enough to terrify the night. As they departed, Brock said to Kerr and me, "If we do not succeed tomorrow at Detroit, the Americans may push us back all the way to Kingston. Victory must be ours."

# 15
## *Detroit, August 1812*

The bombardment of Fort Detroit began early on August 16th. The *Queen Charlotte* had come up river under darkness. Her cannon opened up at dawn. Our battery in Upper Canada, across the river from Detroit, near the little village of Sandwich, followed suit. Each artillery piece could be recognized by the distinctive sound it made. Twelve pounders, a long gun, and mortars could be heard. Soon the American cannon returned fire.

The commencement of guns was our sign to climb into the bateaux and cross the river into the Michigan Territory south of the fort—all seven hundred of us, regulars and militiamen combined. Once on shore we assembled and proceeded along the main road toward our destination. General Brock ordered the drummers to play as loudly as possible so our approach could be heard from some distance. The British were coming and he wanted the Americans to know it.

Although it had rained considerably during the night, the men were in good spirits. We marched in column spread across the roadway. Brock and his staff led the way, followed by the colour party of the 41st with the Union Jack and their yellow regimental flag fluttering in the breeze, the yellow-jacketed drummers banging away, the redcoats with their yellow trim moving in unison, and the militiamen wearing discarded pieces of old uniforms, masquerading as regulars. There was greater space than usual between the rows so that from a distance the force would appear more substantial than it was.

There was no resistance. Our skirmishers found no opposition.

Thirteen years had passed since Holland, the last time I had been in battle. Few of the regulars and none of the militiamen had ever been at war before. The anticipation of glory was energizing.

Nearing the fort, with my telescope I could see American cannon awaiting us, positioned on the road in front of the open gates. No doubt the guns were loaded with grapeshot. That's what I'd have stuffed down the barrels if I were the officer in command. When those sacks exploded, dozens of musket balls would be flung at our column causing terrifying damage. Immediately, I suggested we move from our dusty path, but Brock would not hear of it. "Not yet. We are still out of range. They'll hold their fire a little longer." Then turning in the saddle of one of the horses borrowed from Proctor, he gave instructions to the drummers to intensify their sound.

Brock's safety was of the greatest concern to me as we continued forward. In his famous cocked hat, with gold braid on his uniform dazzling in the morning light, he could not be more visible. "General, perhaps you should not lead the way. Let someone else do it!"

All he said was, "How can I expect my men to go where I am afraid to lead them?"

And we marched on at steady pace. Finally, as we passed through an apple orchard, Brock said as much to himself as anyone, "We've pressed our luck enough," and gave orders for the column to swing to the left. As instructed, the men spread themselves in a long line among the trees. From the fort it would be difficult to tell how many soldiers were hidden from view. The Americans had held their fire; the General had calculated correctly.

From a small depression in the ground on the edge of the orchard the General and I were able to observe our objective. Detroit was a fortified trading post, probably built during the French and Indian War, in the typical style. There were earthen-work ramparts to protect from cannon fire, a ditch to put those who scaled the ramparts beneath men with muskets, and wooden palisades separating four blockhouses holding as many soldiers as possible. Between the fort and the river were perhaps a hundred houses of various descriptions. Meadows and fields of grain, not yet grown to full height, encircled the entire settlement on the other three sides. Beyond that, to the north and west, were boundless, impenetrable forests. There was no discernible activity in the village. The Americans had gone to ground within the fort.

From the forested area came piercing shrieks and war cries. In staggered fashion, warriors darted forward from the trees waving tomahawks and war clubs menacingly, careful to stay out of musket range. Then they retreated to the darkened woods. Brock and Tecumseh had decided that Americans were unlikely to distinguish one Indian from another so the warriors had been instructed on each sortie to reappear from the forest in a different spot from the last. There appeared to be more Indians than the six hundred there actually were.

Brock lowered his telescope and said by way of explanation, "Tecumseh ambushed supply waggons headed for Detroit last week. The American patrol guarding them suffered heavy casualties. This pantomime should remind General Hull of that. The war cries should unnerve him. And a courier of mine was intercepted two days ago. By now Hull should have read my orders to Captain Roberts at Michilimakinac. He'll think Roberts is to bring his five thousand Indians here without delay. If Hull is on edge, this news should push him over the precipice."

Totally perplexed I said, "But Captain Roberts has only three hundred!"

Without looking in my direction he said, "Not five thousand? What a careless mistake."

The artillery barrage went on throughout the morning. Little damage was done to the outer walls. In truth that didn't seem to be the intent. Most of the cannon balls cleared the palisades and hurtled into whatever was in their path as they bounced along within the confines of the fort. Wood, glass, and bones would be shattered. There must have been mayhem within. Some of the mortar fire was hot-shot, cannon balls heated to such a degree that they would ignite whatever they landed upon. Many of these landed in the homes along the riverbank. Smoke rose as the structures were set ablaze.

I must admit that I did have some misgivings. We were assaulting an enemy, twice the size in number, secure within a fort capable of withstanding a siege. It was a bold move. Some might say foolhardy. But I trusted the General completely. His plan was to intimidate the Americans and force Hull into some rash action. Perhaps Brock could draw Hull out of his fortress as Wolfe drew out the French General Montcalm at Quebec fifty years earlier.

In due course Brock summoned an artillery crew that brought forward its one and only rocket. They sent it screaming above the fort for maximum effect before exploding on the other side. The noise it made was unsettling and terrifying. It was also a signal for the Indian excursions and our artillery fire from the river and Upper Canada to stop.

Macdonell and I, with the white flag of truce affixed to my sword, were sent forward with but one instruction. "Pretend that their defeat is a foregone conclusion and our sole aim is to spare them further bloodshed."

About twenty yards from the gate we stopped. I hoped that no one could see the beads of sweat on my forehead. Surely the old barracks tales about enemies shooting messengers couldn't be true. Macdonell called out, "General Hull," as he unrolled the scroll he brought with him. Two officers peered out over the top of the palisades. No doubt they were standing on a walkway behind. One was a grey-haired, old man with gaudy epaulettes on his navy coat. The other was a militia officer, perhaps thirty years of age, robust, wearing on his cocked hat the largest plume I'd ever seen. Macdonell began to read in a voice loud enough for those on and behind the parapet. "A Proclamation to be heard by General Hull and all of the inhabitants of the Michigan Territory under his care. It is far from my intention to participate in your war of extermination. However, should this contest recommence, the Indians who have attached themselves to my command will be beyond my control. Being concerned for the safety of those within this fort, I offer you one opportunity to capitulate. Should you agree to surrender under the terms outlined in this document, no harm will come to anyone. Choose carefully. I will await your immediate response. Sincerely, British Major-General Isaac Brock."

With deliberate slowness, John rolled up the scroll and with arm extended held it out for someone to retrieve it. The American officer with the plume came out, snatched the document with great vehemence, and withdrew. We returned to our lines thankful that no one had prevented us from doing so.

With telescope we were able to watch the silent scene unfolding on the parapet. Their heads and shoulders were clearly visible. The militia officer was livid with rage. Perhaps apoplectic would better describe it. He appeared to be confronting the distraught old man. He waved his arms about, gesturing wildly. Sometimes he'd point in our direction, at others he seemed to be poking General Hull with a finger pointed at his chest. No regular army officer familiar with the court-martial process would dare to speak to a superior officer like that! Not unless he wished to spent the rest of his shortened army career in a stockade. The tirade appeared only to increase the old man's agitation. Finally, the officer with the plume stomped off with exasperation. Shortly after another officer, regular army, with the assistance of a soldier, unfurled a white bed sheet against the outer wall of Fort Detroit. There was complete silence for an instant, followed by exuberant cheering and complete jubilation from the orchard. Only one word came to my mind: 'Victory.'

Eventually Hull, looking very much a broken man, led the officers and men of the U. S. Fourth Infantry from the fort. They tossed their muskets and cartridge belts in piles, and trudged through a gauntlet of redcoats with muskets raised and bayonets affixed. Brock observed from horseback, with Tecumseh astride a magnificent white horse next to him. Glegg was there as well. With as much dignity as he could muster, Hull handed his sword to the General. Another officer presented their regimental colours, the blue national flag bearing the American eagle and the beige silk flag of the Fourth Infantry, to Glegg. Then they marched on, five hundred regulars in all, resigned to their fate. We could smell their humiliation.

John Macdonell, as ranking Canadian militia officer, was given the honour of overseeing the process of paroling nearly two thousand militiamen from Ohio and Kentucky. It was the custom to send militiamen back to their farms, stores, and law practices instead of incurring the expense of keeping them as prisoners of war for the duration . However, paroles carried a condition. Each prisoner was required to swear under oath that he would not fight again unless and until he was exchanged for a paroled militiaman from the other side. For most citizen soldiers a parole meant the war was over for them. I was one of the officers assigned the tasks of taking the oaths and preparing the lists of those paroled, in duplicate. The lines were interminable. Under the watchful eyes of redcoats, disgruntled militiamen deposited their weapons in monstrous piles, shuffled to my table, repeated the oath as stated, said their name, which I transcribed as best I could, and signed next to their name, most with an 'X'. Late in the afternoon, a wild-eyed Kentuckian with unkempt hair and beard, broke from the line, slid a knife from his sleeve where it had been hidden and rushed toward Macdonell sitting on a horse mid parade ground. The assailant raised the knife to strike John in the thigh or stomach, but with startling speed Macdonell drew his pistol from its holster and shot the man in the forehead. Countless Americans readied themselves to fight, but the cocking of redcoat muskets dissuaded them. Macdonell ordered the man to be left motionless on the ground for awhile for all to see before the body was dragged off. The action had a chilling effect on us all.

While the paroling was underway the Indians looted the army buildings and the homes in the village that had not been set ablaze. Nothing could be done to stop it. Horses were especially prized. Tecumseh had promised that no harm would come to either prisoners or civilians, and the warriors obeyed him.

Our success was unimaginable. In one day, with few casualties, we had defeated the U. S. Army of the Northwest. Twenty-five hundred officers and men had been captured. We were in possession of twenty-five hundred muskets, five hundred rifles, thirty-three cannon, tons of invaluable lead and powder, and innumerable supplies. General Brock had accomplished what no one had thought possible.

# 16
## *Niagara, August 1812*

A week later, crowded on board the *Queen Charlotte* and the *Chippawa*, we crossed Lake Erie bound for Niagara with our five hundred prisoners of war. There was scarcely room to move. A small detachment from the 41st accompanied us to assist the York Militia and Norton's band with guarding the Americans. General Brock didn't want anyone reconsidering Hull's promise of surrender. More than a few might have been thinking of taking their chances, jumping in the lake, dodging musket fire, and swimming for shore, but no one tried. The menacing glare of the Indians must have dissuaded them.

We docked at the village of Chippawa, where the ships from the upper lakes unloaded their passengers and cargoes for journey overland around the impassable Niagara Falls. We were expected. Dispatches from Detroit had preceded us. Captain Evers, who ten years previous had been an arrogant young lieutenant familiar with geography, was there to meet us with our own horses, a British flag, and half a dozen drummer boys as the General had requested. A crowd had gathered to welcome us. It wasn't large, but then neither was Chippawa.

Further on, we travelled on roads near enough to hear, but not actually see the water of Niagara cascade from the rock table down into the surging river headed for Lake Ontario.

I imagined the noise to be thunderous applause. Brock must have been thinking the same. He rode along the column of men shouting: "Listen. Imagine that's the roar of the people of the Canadas, celebrating our accomplishments. Never forget it."

In the village of Queenston, where the trail descends the escarpment, larger crowds appeared cheering our success.

Between Queenston and Fort George we marched on the trails nearest the riverbank, a procession for the benefit of anyone in New York State who cared to look. The humbled Fourth Infantry being herded along should have been a discouraging sight. Since receiving the news that they were bound for Quebec and the prison ships anchored in the St. Lawrence River, they were a pretty dispirited lot. General Hull, sequestered in a carriage, dare not show his face, for fear of cruel words from his compatriots. Brock had orchestrated this part of the journey for effect. He said to me, "The Americans have an overrated opinion of their own prowess. This should sow a few seeds of doubt."

Nearing Fort George the General added, "Fitz, it's time for me to play the hero, to animate the loyal." The drummers from the 49th were ordered to play lively tunes on their fifes as we marched. The Church of England steeple bell in Newark announced our arrival. Citizens swarmed from the town to line our pathway. Shopkeepers in their rolled up shirtsleeves, blacksmiths in their leather aprons, lawyers, bankers, and merchants in their suits and high-collared shirts all thrust hands forward wanting to shake a hero's hand and commend him for his endeavours. Brock accepted their compliments graciously and reminded them that he would be needing brave volunteers like them. Their time would come. More than a few responded, "I'll be ready when you need me." Young boys rushed up, just wanting to touch him. Women, young and old, some still with aprons covering their long skirts, spared a few moments from their daily chores. Others dressed up as though going to church service on Sunday handed him flowers as he rode past. Each received a smile for such a warm reception. He neglected no one. One young man balanced on a fence, holding a newspaper so high that its gigantic headline could be seen: 'Victory at Detroit'. Even the local dogs could not contain their excitement, barking enthusiastically as they raced along beside us. I had never witnessed such adulation. Having passed them by, the well-wishers did not disperse but joined in the procession, joyfully chattering among themselves as if this were a parade rather than just an escort for prisoners of war.

The ceremonial cannon fire from the fort added to the tribute.

Before entering the fort, Brock halted the column. He rode back to John Norton and his warriors. I knew that the General had persuaded them to come this far with us before heading home. He said he wanted the Indians to see and be seen. Dismounting, he went to Norton and publicly embraced him, the way comrades might, shaking his hand while placing the other on his shoulder, saying "You have my heartfelt thanks."

Norton replied, "When I tell my Haudenosaunee brothers of all that we have seen and done at Detroit, and of Tecumseh's high regard for you, the Six Nations will commit to this cause. There should be no hesitation when you call us to battle." Then the warriors left for their Grand River homes.

Inside the fort we were honoured with a twenty-one gun salute by a party of regulars. Other members of the 49th, who should have been standing at attention, tossed their shakos skyward in jubilation. While Evers secured the prisoners, Brock approached assembled government dignitaries in front of Officers' Quarters. Aeneas Shaw, Prideaux Selby, and Judge Powell from the Executive Council were easily recognized. More than a few members of the Legislative Assembly, Joseph Willcocks included, were there as well. They had come all the way from York for the occasion. Most wanted to personally congratulate the General, although not everyone did. Willcocks' face seemed to show more scowl than smile. Even General Sheaffe, now in command of Fort George, came up and said, "Well done." Selby encouraged Brock to say some words of inspiration to the soldiers of the garrison and the citizens of Niagara who had followed us into the fort before everyone dispersed. Brock did so. "We are engaged in an awful and eventful contest. We must teach the enemy this lesson: that a country defended by freemen, enthusiastically devoted to the cause of their king and constitution can never be conquered!" At that moment there was no man more admired in the Canadas.

Inside Sheaffe's office over refreshments, the General conversed briefly with each of the dignitaries present. He lingered with Judge Powell and said, "Judge, now that there is support from the citizenry for our cause , we must pass the laws that are required. The assemblymen should not be afraid to vote for them. I need to be able to prosecute anyone guilty of sedition or treason. We can't allow those behind the battlelines to work against us."

"There should be no difficulty achieving this objective now," said Powell.

When all was said and done, the General left with Aeneas Shaw. They were invited to dine in town with his daughter Sophia at the home of Shaw's married daughter, Isabella.

John Macdonell left with his future father-in-law, Judge Powell. As for myself, I went in search of a meal and an empty bed.

# 17
## *Fort George, September 1812*

Glegg and I found General Brock standing at river's edge staring across the shimmering   blue-green water to Fort Niagara with its American flag flapping in the late summer breeze. That morning's dispatch from Prevost was still in his hand. Our approach disrupted his reflection. There was exasperation in his voice when he spoke. "Our momentum is lost. Three weeks have been squandered because of his ill-conceived truce. Sir George informs me the armistice he negotiated with General Dearborn has been rejected by President Madison. He should have known it would be. Now the hostilities will recommence. No doubt the Americans will have used this time to their advantage. They'll have strengthened their positions. Proctor and Tecumseh were not able to attack an unsuspecting Fort Wayne; we were not able to catch the naval base at Sackets Harbour unaware."

"Wouldn't London's promise to end the embargo on American shipping appease them? Was there never any chance of peace, Sir?"

"None at all, Fitz. Prevost remains naive. No country that takes five years to commit itself to war is likely to change its mind after two brief battles. They will not be swayed. Sir George underestimates their animosity. If anything, the humiliation of Detroit has only intensified it. Detroit was only the opening gambit in what surely will be a long and bloody struggle. Niagara will be the next battleground, but where will the invasion come? Fitz, what's your view?"

"Above the falls. At Fort Erie. Not at Chippawa." Pulling a copy of the *Buffalo Gazette* that had been smuggled across the border from my jacket, I gave my reasons. "The press reports military build-up at Black Rock and Buffalo. The information could be false, but I don't believe it is. The people are anticipating success and want to know all the details. The Americans aren't as skilled at deception yet. An attack on Fort Erie would be easier than Chippawa."

The General smiled at my reference to deception, acknowledged this possibility, and asked Glegg for his view.

Glegg replied, "They'll land at Queenston, Sir. Below the falls. I travelled to Lewiston yesterday to arrange for another prisoner exchange, and to get back our men captured with the *schooners Caledonia* and *Detroit*. There are more soldiers milling about every time I go. Even a squad of those half-savage Kentuckians was there."

"Queenston is one of our weakest positions. What about beginning the invasion right here at Fort George, gentlemen?"

"Doubtful," said I. "A sizable proportion of our troops are stationed here. They must anticipate that. Our defences are established."

"Do you think they might feign an attack on one location to draw us out of Fort George or Fort Erie only to overwhelm the position we've just left?"

"It doesn't really matter, General," said Glegg. "We have little to fear from enraged democrats with little subordination or discipline, if you ask me. From what I've seen at their shabby little camp at Lewiston, they're poorly equipped and led by inexperienced amateurs. Some soldiers are without shoes. Morale is poor according to the two deserters who came to us last week; they say their pay is well in arrears. Even the camp is badly arranged. They know nothing of sanitation. The bakers are drawing water for their bread from the river near where the latrines drain into it. Most of the tents they do have are filled with the sick."

"Never underestimate your enemy, John. History is littered with those who made that mistake. Inexperienced or not, there are so many Americans who could take up arms."

"Yes, Sir."

"Our men are spread thinly along the thirty-one miles of river between the two forts. Only six hundred sixty regulars, mostly from the 49th, to defend at least four landing points. We will need to hope for a sign of their intentions."

"One thing is certain," said Glegg. "If there is to be an invasion, it will be soon. Win or lose, the militiamen will want to be on their way home before the snow falls. They're not prepared for a winter encampment."

# 18
## *Queenston Heights, October 1812.*

The deluge had gone on for days. Nothing was dry. Nature's relentless downpour had battered nearly every living thing into submission. The dampness accentuated the cold. Dreariness nearly overwhelmed us. Our sentries all along the Niagara, in army cloaks that protected them as well as anything might, had kept watchful eye, though no enemy activity was anticipated. When gunpowder can't be kept dry, sparks won't ignite and musket and cannon are useless. Then late on the evening of the 12th the rain stopped. Calm silence should have replaced it, but the air crackled with expectation. It was as if the lightening had left residue alerting us to danger.

Earlier in the day Glegg had paddled in a canoe across to Lewiston under the pretext of arranging another prisoner exchange. In contrast to previous excursions, his counterpart wouldn't allow him to disembark. The American officer told him he was too busy to discuss such matters, perhaps in a few days time. Glegg commented to General Brock that the American's demeanour was different; his tone suggested that arranging exchange would be pointless as circumstances were about to change. Hidden in the bulrushes Glegg had seen bateaux, where none had been kept before. The invasion of

Canada was imminent. Brock knew it; Macdonell, Glegg, and I knew it too.

Before leaving Brock's quarters that night, he detained me for a quiet word. "Fitz, I fear I may do something foolish in the days to come. Urge me to caution should this be required." Then winking at me he added, "Allow me to be nothing more than bold."

His request unsettled me, but I quickly reassured the General, "Upon my oath Sir, you can count on me."

That night sleep eluded me for the longest time. When rest did come, anxiety-laden dreams destroyed it. Images of dreadful battle scenes awakened me. I lay in darkness with my own thoughts for most of the night. Whether I actually heard the noise of the cannon, or just sensed it, I do not know. One thing was certain. It had begun.

By the time I had saddled our two horses and arrived at his quarters, the General was outside, fully dressed, issuing instructions to Glegg. "Queenston may still be a diversion. I need to see for myself. John, find General Sheaffe. Tell him to remain here at Fort George with his garrison until the American intent can be determined."

Glegg nodded and set off. Without another word we mounted and rode toward the sound of the cannon.

The rain-ruined, rutted portage road took us through shallow ravines and across swollen, marshy creeks. It was difficult to make haste. Often tree branches formed eery canopies, creating lightless tunnels. Without the wooden rail fences edging our path surely we would have lost our way. The seven mile journey took longer than we hoped.

About dawn we arrived at Vrooman's Point, perhaps a thousand yards down river from Queenston. Two cannon, an eighteen and twelve pounder judging by the size of the balls the artillerymen were ramming down their barrels, were positioned there on river's brink about one hundred twenty feet above the water. The artillerymen were hurriedly going about their duties. A company of York militiamen had come from their campsite nearby to watch the unfolding scene. With telescope in the early light we were able to see a dozen bateaux filled with bluecoats crossing the Niagara, attempting some landing on the gravel of the fishermen's beach just above the village. After depositing their soldiers, they headed back to the original embarkation point near Lewiston on the other side. I quickly calculated that this little flotilla was dropping off nearly three hundred enemy per trip. From the Queenston wharf and warehouse area, incessant volleys were being fired into each bateau by a company of redcoats before the enemy were able to land. The American soldiers could do nothing in reply; there was so little room to move in their boats. Men in each craft could be seen slumped over railings; some leaned against their fellows. When an oarsman was hit another took his place. Canisters filled with musket balls were flung from our sole nine-pounder on the wharf with deadly accuracy. If our men on the docks had all possessed rifles instead of muskets the damage could have been worse. Smoke from our muskets clouded the sky, making it difficult to see where the bluecoats went once they'd jumped ashore. On Queenston Heights, three hundred feet above the village, our big gun pounded the American embarkation point, frequently scattering men before they could board the bateaux when it was their turn to leave. Four American cannon, two smaller in Lewiston itself and two larger from Lewiston Heights, returned fire.

As Brock and I were preparing to leave Vrooman's Point, Macdonell and Glegg caught up to us. The General instructed Macdonell to bring up the militiamen. Before galloping off he attempted to put heart into these civilian soldiers; he waved his sword above his head, and urged them forward, yelling "Push on brave York Volunteers!"

Soon we were in Queenston, the once prosperous village I had visited many times. We rode past the impressive home of the Hamiltons, owners of the cartage business, beyond the inn where coaches stopped on their journey to Fort Erie, past the Secord family's general store, and through the cluster of fine, stone houses along Front Street, to the heart of the battle. Our troops continued their musket fire, not from the docking area where they had been before, but from the edge of the village road leading to the docking area, thirty feet below. Brock sought the man in command. He spied a hatless artillery officer in his royal blue coat, a mixture of grit and sweat marking his face. The explosions were so frequent, the noise so intense, that both had to raise their voices to be heard.

"Captain Dennis, how many have crossed?"

"Don't know, General. They're huddled on the beach, hidden by the bluffs. Whenever one of their boats attempts to land a company appears to engage us, then retreats." Dennis had no sooner explained the tactic when a squad of bluecoats did just that. Several on each side were hit, including Captain Evers, who stumbled and fell forward some way down the sloping road.

"Why have you moved back from the wharf?"

"It was impossible to stay, Sir. Their cannon found our range. Our gun is shattered. I could not afford to lose more men."

Cannon pieces and artillerymen were strewn near the docks, not far from the bodies of numerous, bloodied redcoats. Behind us our army surgeon tended to casualties, several of whom were likely to lose a limb before the day was done.

"You must still have about four hundred men under your command?"

"Yes Sir, about two hundred regulars from the 49th, the light and grenadier companies, and about two hundred militiamen from Lincoln and York. We're spread thinly; some are on the Heights, some here, some near the Point. We'll have difficulty holding the Americans from the village if all those hidden by the bluff make a mad charge, General."

"Understood."

At this point the Americans changed their tactics. Three bateaux reloaded with bluecoats were drifting downstream with the current towards Hamilton Cove. Observing this, Brock made a quick assessment of our situation and began issuing orders.

"Captain Glegg, bring the squad of men from the Heights down into the village. No one can reach the Heights without passing through here. Captain Dennis, take a squad of men from the village to Hamilton Cove. You must prevent the enemy establishing a second landing.

We mustn't be outflanked. Lieutenant FitzGibbon, ride back to Fort George. Give my instructions to General Sheaffe. He is to come here with all due speed. Should you pass Macdonell, inform him that he is ordered to join Captain Dennis. I'll remain here."

"But Sir...," I stammered, not wanting to leave Brock.

"Hurry, Fitz."

"Yes, General." There was little else I could do.

After relaying the General's summons to Sheaffe, I switched horses and returned to Queenston. The trip was much faster in daylight. I stopped at Hamilton Cove to receive news from Captain Dennis. He could not contain his satisfaction.

"Success, FitzGibbon! Success! We positioned ourselves here at the foot of this garden, and raked their boats with murderous fire from atop this bluff. Look! They're shattered!"

Below were two beached bateaux. A dozen soldiers lay still in the poses of the dead. On the narrow shale shore perhaps thirty wounded were spread out awaiting some attention. Those who surrendered were being marched up the path to the top of the bluff.

"Only one bateau was able to escape," continued Dennis. "There were scarcely enough survivors to row. Macdonell and the militiamen have gone on."

"Excellent results, Captain. I'll be sure to inform the General if Lieutenant-Colonel Macdonell has not done so already." With great enthusiasm I rode on.

In the village there was more desperation than I'd antici-pated. The firefight near the wharf still raged on. Bluecoat numbers had increased; ours seemed to have diminished. Glegg was overseeing the distribution of ammunition. Soldiers were opening their leather pouches to accept more cartridges. Their first lot of sixty must have been used. Soon the muskets would be too hot to touch. "Where's General Brock?"

"There," said Glegg, pointing to a stone wall at the bottom of the Heights.

Crouching behind it were the General and perhaps seventy soldiers, half redcoats, half militiamen.

"Why is he there?"

"The Americans have taken the Heights."

"What?"

"Somehow, unseen, they ascended the Heights. They must have hauled themselves up grasping young trees and bushes as they climbed. Then they came out of the woods on top behind the guns. The artillerymen had just enough time to disable the cannon before running away. All this was reported to the General."

"How many are up there?"

"We don't know. The General is furious that he ordered the squad down from there."

"Don't tell me he intends to regain the lost ground!"

"I counselled against it, Fitz. He wouldn't listen. I advised him to wait for Sheaffe's reinforcements. He just got that look of his and replied that a counter attack with a platoon now would be better than a counter attack in two hours with a full brigade."

"Glegg, a frontal attack, uphill, over open ground against an enemy of unknown strength can't go well. He must be dissuaded."

Before I could get to him, General Brock jumped to the top of the wall, raised his sword, screamed something I was too far away to hear, perhaps 'Follow me', and led the charge up Queenston Heights over barren ground, as the hill had been cleared of trees to give better sight lines for the cannon. American militiamen, now visible, stepped forward, took aim, and fired. A ball must have nicked Brock's hand. He jerked it sharply, and shook it once or twice, but this did not slow his pace. He had just half-turned to urge the men on when he stopped as though something had slammed into his chest. Slowly he sank down, tumbling onto his left side. The charge continued. Seeing what had happened, a few men stood and knelt in front of the General to shield him from further injury. Private O'Byrne was one. A moment later he crumpled and fell at Brock's feet. A young militiaman, a boy no more than fifteen, attempted to prop up the General and speak to him. By the time I'd reached them the General's eyes were already closed. The boy looked directly at me and said, "I asked the General if he was very much hurt, but he gave no reply." The small hole in his jacket not far from his heart told me all that I needed to know. I couldn't speak. Only one thought filled my mind: 'get him to safety,' as though that mattered. With help from the boy and a redcoat, we lifted him back behind the stone wall. I sat next to him in shock, unable to move, as the realization set in. Our leader, was dead.

The charge did not push the Americans from the Heights. Our men retreated to behind the wall where they had begun.

Macdonell atop his horse appeared from somewhere. He saw Brock's lifeless body and looked to me with hopeful eyes seeking affirmation. Instead, slowly shaking my head from side to side, I confirmed his fears. John looked skyward. Some great growl came from deep within his being. He forced the horse over the wall in one bound and galloped along the length of the fencing shouting, "Avenge the General." This rallied the men who began a second attack from the bottom of the hill. Their charge was ferocious. It took me a few moments to shake off my paralysis. I joined in, only to see Macdonell go down. A ball must have hit his horse. It reared up in pain and twisted, exposing John's back. Another musket ball must have entered there. Both horse and rider plunged forward. Macdonell was thrown over the animal's head and lay motionless. Blood flowed from his stomach where the ball exited, and other places as well. He must have been shot more than once. With assistance I dragged him back behind the wall. His pain must have been intense; he opened his eyes and whispered, "Help me." I found the surgeon to treat his wounds. The second attack failed. It was only about 8:00 a.m.

For sometime thereafter, nothing happened. The Americans in superior numbers did not pour down from the Heights to overpower us. We expected they would. We had no idea why they didn't. Nor did we know how many there were. Necessary tasks distracted me from my grief. Glegg and I moved the General's body to the inn, and Macdonell back to the surgeon's tent on the river road. The entire force was withdrawn to Dennis' position near the Hamilton house. We braced ourselves. More Americans should have been crossing the Niagara, but they weren't. There was nothing to stop them. Through my field glasses I could see commotion at Lewiston. New York Militiamen appeared to be resisting all attempts to force them into the boats. If this continued, only the army on the Heights need be confronted - perhaps from behind. General Sheaffe needed to be in possession of this information so I set off to find him.

Sheaffe was appreciative of my report on all that had transpired. He took his column, about eight hundred in all, half regulars from the 41st, on the three mile detour around Queenston through farmland to catch the enemy unaware on the Heights from behind. As we neared, war whoops and skirmishing fire aplenty could be heard on the Heights at the back of the sloping hill where Brock had been shot. Behind the placement of the spiked cannon, edging the escarpment on the river side and spreading out away from the hill were woods. Using the trees to protect themselves, John Norton's Mohawks harassed the bluecoats. There were many more Americans than we had expected, but they were poorly formed. Some units faced down the slope, perhaps readying themselves for another charge from below; some faced in the opposite direction preoccupied by the menacing musket fire of the Mohawks; some just milled about awaiting some order.

Sheaffe approached through the farm fields opposite the river. He set his men as he wished: regulars, Lincoln Militiamen, and Captain Runcey's Coloured Corp of about three dozen with their own score to settle. We spread out across the field in visible lines with bayonets affixed. We followed Sheaffe's direction, "Let's show them what we're made of." To the slow, intimidating beat of the drum, we moved forward. Hurriedly the Americans formed and turned to receive us. Warriors continued to snipe at their flank. About fifty yards from their position we stopped, and as ordered fired one mass volley. Then with bayonets gleaming in the mid-afternoon sun, we charged their line. Myself, I was so filled with hate that I intended to kill until I was too weary to lift my sword. God help me.

There was no resistance. Our bayonet charge unnerved their amateur army. Most broke and ran for the woods; those who stood their ground suffered for their courage. Skirmishing in the woods slowed our advance, but we pushed them back to the edge of the escarpment overlooking the river. They could go no further. Piercing shrieks told us the few who tried to retrace their steps and descend the steep embankment lost their grip and plunged into the swirling Niagara. The Americans weren't willing to die on Queenston Heights. White flags appeared. New York Militia General William Wadsworth with U. S. Artillery Colonel Winfield Scott at his side surrendered another American army. It was late afternoon on October 13th.

Duties kept me preoccupied until dusk. Prisoners had to be secured, weapons collected, and casualties moved to where they could receive medical attention. The dead were removed from the field of battle, and food brought forward for the living. When all this was done I slipped away from our encampment into the darkness and wept for my friends.

# 19
## *Fort George, October 1812*

With morning light I set out for the army hospital in search of John Macdonell. The weather-beaten, faded canvas tent was beyond the village on the river road. Opening the flap I looked upon an exhausted man in a blood-drenched apron, sweat on his bald head glistening from the light of the oil lamp hung above. He held an amputation saw in one hand, a severed arm in the other. Next to him on a makeshift table lay a soldier pinned by a short, powerfully built orderly in spattered clothing. Recognizing that the patient was no longer conscious, passing out from pain no doubt, the orderly released his grip. The soldier's torment might just be beginning, but at least he wouldn't be dying from the killing gangrene. The surgeon turned to see who was entering.

"What do you want, FitzGibbon?" he asked, tossing the arm across the darkened, straw-covered ground to the box in the corner overflowing with other limbs.

"Sorry to disturb you, Sir. The whereabouts of Lieutenant-Colonel Macdonell, would you know it?"

"Back in the village. Those recovering from surgery are in a house. The one with the green door."

"Thank you. Are you aware of his condition?"

He shook his head from side to side, wiped his saw with a torn piece of cloth, and placed it on a little table holding his instruments before retrieving the needle and thread he'd need to sew a long, dangling piece of skin over the bloody stump before him.

As I left I heard his assistant say, "Daylight, Sir. No need to fret about night vapours now."

In Queenston there was no uncertainty about which house held the casualties. Groans and gentle moaning could be heard in the street. The smell of death and dying assaulted the senses as I stepped through the door. Bodies lay everywhere on beds of straw covered by army blankets; they were in the hall, in the parlour to the left, and kitchen to the right. Furniture was piled on the edges of each room to allow more space on the floor. There was barely enough room to move among the suffering: men with bandaged eyes and heads, those with severed hands, arms, feet and legs, men with foul stomach wounds not long for this earth. There were redcoats and militiamen. Pain treated them all alike. In the centre hall near the stairs to the second floor, a young woman with tears quietly rolling down her cheeks knelt next to a man, holding his hand. Recognizing my distress at being unable to find the man I sought, she pointed above and said, "There's a few more upstairs."

On a bed in what must have been the children's room I found John. His eyes were closed. Not wanting to startle him from sleep I softly called his name. There was no response. His eyes did not open. Hoping to find a pulse I touched his neck, and felt only the cold clamminess of death. John Macdonell's eyes would be sightless forever. At his bedside, using words my mother had taught me all those years ago, I prayed for him. There were no more tears to shed.

Plans had already been made to transport Isaac Brock's body to Fort George for burial. I arranged for Macdonell to be loaded into the same waggon. The route was the same we'd travelled in triumph less than two months earlier—lifetimes ago. At intervals we passed through crowds of people, soldiers and citizens. Redcoats stood stiffly at attention, saluting to show admiration and respect for their General. Militiamen with hats removed, jaws clenched in solemn determination, bowed their heads for their leader. Ordinary people, who had somehow learned the body was being moved, lined the roadside, men with hand on heart, women sniffling into handkerchiefs, mourning their hero. Myself, I struggled to feel nothing at all.

Upon arriving at Fort George I reported immediately to General Sheaffe. Having returned from Queenston Heights he had settled into the comfort of his quarters. He appeared to be preparing an account of events for Quebec or London, one that emphasized his accomplishments I was sure. With hat tucked under my arm, I stood at attention in front of his desk. His mood was jubilant.

"What a glorious victory, eh FitzGibbon! Another American army subdued and captured!"

Selecting a piece of paper from those scattered before him on the desk he read, "Captured seventy-one officers and eight hundred fifty-three soldiers. Nearly a thousand. Four hundred thirty-six are regulars from the U.S. Thirteenth and Twenty-third Infantries. Four hundred eighty-nine are militiamen. We'll need to arrange their parole. Difficult to determine how many casualties they have. Some returned to Lewiston in those boats; some bodies were carried away by the Niagara. At least two hundred, perhaps as many as five hundred."

"Yes, Sir. We held our ground."

"And our own casualties are minimal." Finding another piece of paper on the desk he added, "Twenty dead and eighty-five wounded. Norton says of his warriors, five were killed and nine wounded." Sheaffe caught the twitch of my eye when he'd mentioned the 'minimal damage' that had been done. "Unfortunate about General Brock and Lieutenant-Colonel

Macdonell. Senior officers shouldn't be leading infantry charges."

At that moment I wanted to smash his face to a bloody pulp. He had so little regard for the lives of my friends. But I did nothing. I knew what the consequences of such an ill-considered action would be: court-martial and firing squad.

General Sheaffe studied me carefully for the longest time.

"You will need reassignment, FitzGibbon. Your services as adjutant are no longer required. Let me give some thought to this matter."

"Sir, may I have your permission to inform Miss Shaw of the burial arrangements?"

"Permission granted. You are dismissed, Lieutenant."

Before I was through her sister's garden gate, Miss Sophia burst from the house, distraught. She threw her arms around me and held on as though I was the only one who could keep some undertow from pulling her under and drowning her. "Fitz, tell me it's not true! My Isaac! Tell me there has been some dreadful mistake. Tell me he's not dead."

I wished I could.

# 20
## *Kingston, January 1813*

My new assignment, the one General Sheaffe thought appropriate, was to bring a convoy of supplies from Kingston to Fort George by sleigh in the midst of a brutal Canadian winter. Perhaps I should have been angry with him. In truth, I was so despondent over recent events that I did not much care where Sheaffe sent me or what he asked me to do.

By New Year's Eve I found my way to the fortified harbour town on the eastern end of Lake Ontario. Kingston was the principal British naval base in Upper Canada and comparable in size to York and Newark. With the control of the lakes being so essential to the defence of the country, it was of vital importance. Sackets Harbour, the main American naval base, was only thirty-five miles away on Ontario's southern shore. I had been in Kingston briefly a decade earlier when the 49th passed through on its way from Quebec to Niagara. The town still had a very lively feel to it. Merchants, naval officers, and sailors bustled about, undaunted by the cold. Carpenters banged away on their latest creation in the dockyards. Everyone readied themselves for the day when the ice on the lake would melt, freeing the combatants from their respective harbours.

There was no room for me in the officers' quarters in the fort. Naval officers preferring to spend little time on their frigid ships in the harbour filled the empty beds. Instead, alternate arrangements were made for me at a respectable inn on the edge of town on the coach road. I was much impressed with the accommodation. The Loyalist was a two-storey brick structure built after the latest fashion. The front door opened onto a centre hall. To the left there was a room large enough to serve as a tavern for thirsty travellers and neighbouring farmers in search of good company, freed by winter from some of their daily chores. To the right was a dining area with tables and chairs, and a settee in front of the fireplace for any women wishing to take rest during their stay. A substantial kitchen was positioned across the back. Delicious scents filled each room and mingled where the spaces met: pine from the Christmas boughs still decorating the hall, cinnamon wafting from the kitchen, lavender from the dining room, and the smell of whatever spices were used in the mulled cider warming on the bar. On the second floor were half-a-dozen sleeping rooms with most comfortable beds, and I can attest to that. The owner was a plump, jovial man with bushy grey hair and eyebrows, most suited for his occupation. William Haley was his name. Haley greeted each guest with welcoming words, like some lost friend he had just found. He happily engaged everyone in conversation and entertained them with his endless repertoire of amusing stories. The mistress of the kitchen and the dining room was his daughter, Mary. Fully expecting someone accustomed to the enjoyment of her own cooking, I was pleasantly surprised to find a remarkable young woman, handsome in both face and figure. There was a brother as well, a shy young lad who tended the stable, set behind the brick cottage next door where the family resided. He appeared only when firewood was needed to warm the inn.

Initially I devoted myself to military matters, spending little time at The Loyalist. My task required considerable preparation and planning. Commissary officers assisted me in procuring the items necessary: sleighs, teams of horses in equal number to the sleighs, toboggans easily attached to the sleighs, winter tents, blankets, axes for chopping firewood, army great coats, mitts, scarves for protecting ears, winter moccasins like the aboriginals wore, and snowshoes. The goods requested for the garrison at Fort George also had to be assembled: ammunition, rum sufficient for the daily rations, and foodstuffs—flour, potatoes, and salted pork. The two hundred and fifty mile trip had to be carefully mapped out. Our horses required food and shelter. There was no point in self-deception; it would not be easy for the army to replace the escorts, but the animals would be even more difficult to replace. Without the horses there would be no convoy at all. Should inns and supportive farmers be unable to provide for them, we'd need to load up the toboggans and bring fodder along for them.

After two weeks, the bulk of the work was done and I was able to take my evening meal at The Loyalist. Miss Haley's savoury stews, succulent roast chicken, and apple pies were beyond compare. She served the guests herself. Whenever I thought she might not notice I watched as she moved about the tables with such grace. Like her father she had a way with people. She enquired about the details of their journey, charmed them with compliments on some item of apparel or appearance, and asked for their views on matters of importance in the province. If asked for her own views, her thoughts showed perspective and good sense. She had a sense of fun as well and lightened the journey of more than one weary traveller. There was a healthy glow to her. I'd never fancied 'society' beauties with their pale complexions, alerting prospective suitors to families prosperous enough to keep them from exertion and the sun.

Just before my little expedition was scheduled to depart, a winter storm descended upon Kingston. Punishing winds from the northwest battered the town. Tiny pellets of ice stung the eyes and pinged off window glass. Ice turned to snow. Angry swirling winds hurled it into anything standing in its way—hedges, houses, and comfortable little inns—piling it in great drifts. Hour after hour the storm continued until at least two feet of snow blanketed the ground. Finally it dissipated. Nothing could be done until the roads became passable. So, journey delayed, I sat alone in the dining room, and by the gentle light of the fire, read the last book General Brock had loaned me.

Lost in thought, I did not notice her until I looked up and saw Mary sitting across from me at my table. A strand of that wavy red hair escaped from the tie at the back and fell across her face. She tried to brush it back with her hand.

"James FitzGibbon, are you reading one of those English romance novels I've heard so much about?"

I could see the mischief in those sparkling blue eyes.

"I'm done with those stories of moors, manor houses, and unrequited love. Thought I'd read this instead."

With amusement she asked, "What's this one about then?"

"It's a story of a man havin' great difficulty gettin' home after the Trojan War."

"I'm sure you'd be finding your way home. Where is home if you don't mind a girl asking?"

"As you can probably tell from this charmin' accent you're hearing, I was born in Ireland. My home? That's an entirely different question. Until a few months ago I'd have said the army. Not so sure anymore. Perhaps it still is. How long have you been here?"

"All my life. This is my home. Father and mother came here from New York when the patriots chased them out. Fortunately father had enough put aside to bring with him and establish himself here in Upper Canada. He's proud of the choice he made. The name of the inn makes it clear to all."

"Were you born here in Kingston?"

"I was, my younger brother and I, but I worry about our future here. What uncertainty this war brings! Will we be dislodged by the Americans? Father is too old to begin again. What do you think will happen, Lieutenant?"

"I don't know Miss. Too soon to tell. A year ago hardly anyone thought resisting an invasion was possible. Then came Detroit and Queenston Heights. I'll never forget the determination set in the faces of the militiamen after Queenston."

"Did you ever meet General Brock?"

"For the past eight years I served as his adjutant. He was my friend."

Until that moment I had not realized how much I needed to share my experiences, and proceeded to do so. I told Mary Haley the story of my life. She listened most attentively, enquiring about this and that. When I was done I asked about her life. She told me of her grief when her mother passed away, her fears, and the trials and tribulations of owning an inn. Our conversation lasted for hours.

Finally, she rose to begin preparations for dinner. "I'm truly sorry about the death of your friend, James. I'll tell you what I believe. With our passing each of us leaves a legacy. The legacy lives as long as the memories of the person remains in the hearts and minds of others. Isaac Brock will leave quite a legacy." Her words affected me most profoundly.

Over the next few days we talked often. When it was time to depart I asked, "Miss Haley, may I write to you?"

All she said was, "I'd be most disappointed if you didn't, Lieutenant FitzGibbon."

When the convoy of sleighs left Kingston the weather was agreeable. The sky was a brilliant blue. The sunlight sparkled on the snow so brightly that eyes sometimes needed shielding. The air was fresh and exhilarating. Pines, cedars, and balsam bent under the pure white covering, but none were broken by the burden. It seemed a winter paradise.

We made excellent time until the fourth day when harsh northern winds returned. The temperature dropped. The air was so chill that it stung the lungs. Breathing pained the chest.

Frost encrusted whiskers, eyebrows and eyelashes. Though we huddled on the seats of our sleighs, wrapped in buffalo robes, the cold still penetrated. At times we could not stop from shuddering. For more than a week we soldiered on without another thought of paradise.

Despite the hardship every moment was not a misery. At night we reached a campsite prepared by the advanced party. Tents would be up. Bubbling kettles filled with potatoes would be hung over warm, blazing fires. Fish, caught through holes in the lake ice, were stuck on sticks and ready for roasting in the fire. A ration of rum reminded men of their favourite stories. There was a camaraderie among us that only such experience can bring. Then when we turned in there was a stillness unlike any I'd ever known. A silence that had been heard for a thousand years made it easy to forget the urgency and chaos of war.

Eventually we passed the barren trees and bushes glittering with silvery frost on the outskirts of Fort George. With my spirit renewed, we reached our destination.

# 21
## *Fort George, May 1813*

In Spring there was glorious news from the west. The combined forces of Colonel Proctor and Tecumseh had crossed into the Michigan Territory and surprised General Winchester's army at Frenchtown on the River Raisin. Winchester's army was destroyed; the damage done to the Americans was severe. The mood at Fort George was most optimistic. That changed in a flash in late April.

From where I was on patrol I could see it clearly. The red-orange discolouration appeared in the distance, framed by the brilliant blue of Ontario's water and the paler tones of the sky. About two minutes later thunder rolled across the lake. Startled birds ceased their singing and took flight. Guard's ears perked up; without command he halted. Then the air over the calm waters shimmered in the mid-day sun and whispered warning as it blew past on its way to rattle the windows in town. I searched the horizon for some explanation. Perhaps a grand naval battle had just begun and more volleys would follow, but I could see none. There was only silence. The sight and sound had come from the direction on York, a mere twenty- eight miles across the lake. Gradually the idea came to me. Just one thing could have caused such an explosion: the powder magazine at Fort York had ignited! And only retreating armies destroyed their powder to keep it from falling into enemy hands.

Within days our camp was jolted by the stories brought from occupied York. The Americans had arrived from Sackets Harbour in a small armada. General Sheaffe had not prevented their landing; he had abandoned the provincial capital and was last seen leading his army toward Kingston. When the powder exploded, tons of stone and timber were launched into the sky. The debris fell to earth pummelling General Pike and his vanguard; hundreds of U.S. soldiers were dead. Bluecoats set the parliament buildings ablaze and looting was widespread. The Americans ransacked empty homes. Wives of militiamen gone with Sheaffe could not stop the enemy from seizing anything they could find. Money and valued possessions could be hidden, but some things had to be left in plain sight. Food of any description was taken. To make matters worse, enemy sympathizers within the community began to show themselves, readily surrendering and requesting paroles that would free them from participation in the conflict, even volunteering to help the occupiers. Everyone wondered when the armada would set sail for Niagara. Bleak seemed the best word to describe our circumstance.

We waited on alert for several weeks. General John Vincent was now in command at Fort George; he'd succeeded Sheaffe, who'd become chief administrator in the province with Brock's death. Vincent was Anglo-Irish and a professional soldier; he was experienced and generally liked for the decent treatment of his men, but there was no edge to his sword. There were only a thousand regulars and three hundred militia under his command, hardly enough to defend Niagara with us scattered between the lake and Queenston Heights. I'd been given a company of the 49th to lead. We were positioned on the Heights should the enemy try to cross the river there a second time.

On May 27th, following a week of driving rain and turbulent winds, on a morning so foggy we couldn't see fifty yards ahead of us, the enemy attack finally began. From the sound of the guns there was action at Fort George, and perhaps on the lake shore beyond the town. My lads wished to join in, but we awaited our orders. About noon as the fog lifted we observed the small band of warriors under Norton's command slipping away. Then an express rider galloped in our direction. To help stop the agitated horse I grasped the bridle and questioned the messenger.

"What news, soldier?"

"Are you Lieutenant FitzGibbon?"

When I assured him I was, he began to fumble through letters in his pouch. "I have orders from General Vincent."

"Forget the paper for a minute, man! Tell me what's happening."

He stopped what he'd been doing and gave me his full attention. "We are overwhelmed, Sir! An immediate retreat has been ordered. Your instructions are in this letter from General Vincent." He resumed the search of his pouch until he found what he'd been seeking and handed it to me. "I'm off to Fort Erie. Lieutenant-Colonel Bisshopp is to leave the fort and rendez-vous with you."

"We're abandoning Niagara?"

"Afraid so, Sir."

In total disbelief we departed the Queenston Heights in haste. By nightfall my company had reached a place on the escarpment covered with ponds and marshes, known as Beaver Dams. Other units assembled there as well. A quick count was taken. Nearly a third of Vincent's force, three hundred fifty regulars and eighty-five militiamen, were missing, killed, wounded, or captured. Bisshopp's men bolstered our numbers when they arrived. With only a few hours rest, we set off on the road to York, fearing the Americans were in close pursuit. Did it ever stop raining that Spring? In incessant drizzle we trudged along muddy roads through countless small ravines and forded the numerous swollen rivulets that flowed from the escarpment to the lake below, destroying bridges as we went. Past Twenty Mile Creek, and Forty Mile Creek, and Stoney Creek we tramped, until two days later we stopped at the spot it appeared we'd be making a stand, at Burlington Heights, on the narrow strip of land that separated the bay at the western end of the lake from the marshy waters of Cootes Paradise.

# 22
## *Stoney Creek, June 1813*

"Who goes there?" demanded the young American in a uniform too big for his frame. Sentries had been posted in the woods on the edge of the farms beside Stoney Creek. This one was positioned in the wood lot facing west, not far from the plank-board church with the beginnings of a cemetery next to it. I'd startled him. He raised his musket nervously, trying desperately to assess the threat I posed.

Wearing settler's clothes and making no effort to conceal myself, I replied in an Irish accent so exaggerated he'd never mistake me for an Englishman, "A welcome sight for a hungry man, I am." I approached him with my basket held up with two hands so that he could see I carried no weapon. Stopping a couple of yards away, I tipped it slightly toward him. "Look. Butter. That's what I've come to sell: butter and a few loaves of bread."

The sentry lowered his musket a few inches away from his face so he could get a better view of the two dozen small blocks of butter spread out on leaves on the bottom of my woven basket.

"Wouldn't a layer of delicious butter spread thickly over a slice or two of bread warm from its pan make a grand supper!

Can't you just taste it? You'll never hear a better price than the one I'm askin'."

By the way he wet his lips, he could easily imagine each savoury mouthful.

"Does the army feed you so well you're not hungry, lad?"

Grumpily he replied, "I'm hungry enough. Haven't had a meal to fill my belly since we left Fort George. But I've no money. Haven't received the pay we've been promised."

"Sorry to hear that. Perhaps your company cook might have funds to purchase my wares? I'd prefer to see good men like yourself benefit from my service."

"Cook won't have any money."

"Point me in his direction. I'll give him first chance to buy. If he can't, well I'll offer this butter to the officers. They always have a few coins to satisfy their appetites."

"The officers already eat better than me. Besides, I've not been given orders about lettin' peddlers into camp."

"You won't be denying a man an opportunity for a little commerce, will you? Having a few American coins in my pocket will be handy when you lads win this war and send the British back where they came from."

The musket lowered a little more.

"Perhaps we could strike a bargain. Come to an agreement, you and me. Let me pass and I'll give you a block of butter and half a loaf of bread just for helpin' me on my entrepreneurial way. What do ya say? Find someone in a fancy uniform and get permission if that's all you'd be needin'."

"Can't leave my post."

"Right you are. Hmm. Perhaps if you knew someone who could vouch for my good intentions. Do you know my cousin? Friends tell me he's marchin' with this army of yours. Willcocks. Joseph Willcocks is his name. Bit a dandy is our Joseph. Have you met him? Fine suit. Emerald green sash across his chest. Similar band on his top hat. Smile big enough to impress the ladies."

"I might have seen a man like that, talking to General Winder by the farm house, but I don't know him."

"No need for worrying then. Let me pass. If anyone stops me I'll say Cousin Joseph has sent for me. No risk to you. How can fattening up a general or two be amiss?"

Dropping his gun to waist height, he said, "Offer me two blocks of butter and a whole loaf of bread."

"Done. You drive a hard bargain. You won't be regrettin' this decision."

With the stock of his musket on the ground the boy reached out to grasp what I'd promised. Both of us were smiling.

On the eastern edge of the wood I crouched in bushes and unwrapped my field glass from the leafy covering on the bottom of my basket. Laying flat on the ground I observed the enemy encampment. Before dusk there was still light enough to see. The site was not unfamiliar to me; we'd marched through in retreat to Burlington Heights. Situated in a saucer-shaped meadow about two hundred yards wide were a couple of prosperous little farms. The meadow was rimmed on both sides with earthen embankments, fifteen to twenty feet high, covered in brush, with fallen timbers and young saplings poking out. A rocky brook carried May rains from the forested escarpment to my right down to Lake Ontario on my left, perhaps a mile in the distance. Gently swaying grain filled most of the little valley, but there was grassland as well where lazy cattle grazed. The Queenston Road going across split the meadow, separating two log cabins, about a hundred yards apart. The cabin on the foothills below the escarpment must have been commandeered for the generals, judging by the number of officers milling about. Not far from the creek, army cooks were setting up the frames to support their black cauldrons. Soldiers, with jackets removed because of the heat still oppressive late in the evening, took apart carefully assembled rail fences, gathering firewood. Waggons rumbled up the laneway connecting the cabins, perhaps bringing supplies from boats on the lake. To my dismay the landscape, the meadow and the ridge across, was filled with soldiers, most in their navy jackets and white pants, but some wearing coats dyed light brown or greyish brown. Tents were set up in random fashion. Regiments seemed to establish themselves where ever they wished, not in battle formation in anticipation of a surprise enemy attack. Some regiments bedded down near the line of cooks; some were on the ridge; some chose the orchard behind the command centre. Most noticeable were four artillery pieces blocking the road on the far rim. Surely the Americans must have brought more, but they were not ready for action.

Stealthily I by-passed my satiated friend on his piquet and returned to share my observations with Vincent's second in command. Lieutenant-Colonel John Harvey was younger than Vincent, and there was a bit of dash to him. Camp gossip told of his journey from Halifax: one hundred sixty miles of it in snowshoes, moving at quick pace so he wouldn't be late for the fight, he reached Fort George in twenty-eight days. It was hard not to admire a man for that. With John Norton and a handful of dragoons on horseback, he waited for my report near Davis' Tavern atop the hill of red earth above Big Creek, about half a mile away.

"What's the disposition of the enemy, FitzGibbon?" he asked as soon as I was near enough to hear.

"They outnumber us, Sir. At a guess, two to one. They're settling in for the night and don't expect to be disturbed. The forward regiments are set up by the cooks' fires; they're easily seen in the firelight. If they move on Burlington Heights tomorrow we'll have a hard time holding them back."

"What are you proposing, Lieutenant? A surprise attack tonight?"

"I am, Sir."

"There's merit to your idea. Supplies are low. Our soldiers have no more than the ammunition in their cartridge boxes.

Our cannon will be done in ten minutes. A prolonged battle will not go in our favour. Norton, what do you think?"

His simple reply, "Attack", did not surprise me. Warriors always preferred to surprise their opponents.

"Quite a gamble, gentlemen."

"Colonel Harvey, if we can't hold the Burlington Heights, we'll be forced back to Kingston. Proctor and Tecumseh will be isolated at Amherstberg and easily outflanked. The entire province is at risk."

The night was uncommonly dark. Cloud cover had snuffed out the moon and stars. Harvey moved a few paces off into the stillness of the night and stood motionless. Eventually he turned. "There's a time for caution and a time for daring. Dragoon, return to General Vincent. Convey this to him. It is my wish that he bring our forces forward now. I will await him here."

We watched the dragoon disappear into the blackness. I feared that if he ever strayed from the Queenston Road he'd lose his way. About an hour later our messenger returned to relay General Vincent's response. Upon hearing that the General declined such a rash action Harvey gritted his teeth and instructed us to wait where we were while the Colonel returned to the Burlington Heights himself. We did not see or hear from him for another two hours when he reappeared with a large contingent moving as quietly as they could.

"Gentlemen, General Vincent has reconsidered. In part. He has agreed to the plan and placed half his force at my command, about eight hundred men, five companies from the 49th and five companies from the 8th. Our chances will be decent if we can maintain surprise."

I agreed fully with him. It was now June 6th, about 1:30 a.m. according to Harvey's timepiece.

Harvey's plan was simple enough. After silencing the sentries, we would move quickly through the woods and attack with bayonets. While the front line slept by the campfires we'd dispatch them and cause enough commotion to frighten the rest away. Untested American soldiers, unaccustomed to hand-to-hand combat, would scatter fearing nasty bayonet wounds that never healed easily. The 8th was to charge the command post, the log cabin belonging to James Gage, on the escarpment side of the Queenston Road, while the 49th attacked on the lake side of it. To ensure the element of surprise, the Colonel ordered all flints be removed so that no accidental shot might be fired; without flint no spark could ignite the powder in the musket pan should nervousness cause a trigger be pulled, ending the silence.

Only the first part of our plan was executed as intended. Norton's warriors and a few of us volunteered to dispatch the sentries, killing or capturing them as we saw fit. I agreed to silence the boy I'd deceived earlier that evening.

About ten yards from where I remembered him to be, in a sing-song voice I called out, "Butter man!" I must have startled him again.

"Who....who goes there?" he stammered.

"It's the butter man, you daft lad. Were you not listening? I just told you."

"Advance and be recognized."

"I've brought you a gift. Just wanted to thank you for assisting me with my commerce. I'd like to make arrangements with you for tomorrow."

Because of the impenetrable darkness he couldn't see me until I was practically upon him. The first thing he saw was the loaf of bread extended in my left hand. He rested his musket and reached out to accept it. Then looking down he noticed my army boots. When he'd seen me at dusk I'd been in my peddler's costume, but I'd thought the darkness would disguise my officer's shirt and pants well enough for my purpose. The boots gave me away. As he looked up in disbelief and was about to alert his fellows, I slugged him on the jaw with all my might. He fell backwards and lay there in a heap. I tied and gagged the lad with rope and cloth I'd left in the bushes behind. There was no need to do more than was required. My lad was luckier than most. Many a piquet departed this earth that night, especially the the ones who had abandoned their posts for a few hours sleep in the little Methodist church.

In the deepest part of the night our force moved forward with stealth to confront the regiment sleeping by the camp-fires. To our surprise they were gone. Only the cooks and bakers remained. Then the unforgivable happened. From where a group of officers were stationed excited "huzzas" and mimicked war cries broke the complete silence that hung over the meadow. Shouts of alert from the enemy position fol-lowed. Sounds of soldiers rousing themselves for battle stung us. I believe I could have killed the idiots who'd disobeyed Colonel Harvey's orders myself if they had been nearer. Our situation was unimaginably poor. The advantage of surprise was lost. Only the cooks had been over whelmed. Some enemy units must have been where we expected them to be because fighting began to the left and to the right, but in the middle the bulk of the front line had disappeared to God knew where. Moreover, the campfires illuminated our presence. American musket fire, which began in scattered fashion, increased in intensity. At least the muzzle flash of their guns gave their posi-tion away. Punishing fire continued from the embankment. Commands were barked out to our men: "Douse the fires," and "Replace your flints." Some began to fall about me. The rest of my men were frozen in uncertainty, awaiting my instruc-tion. I hesitated. All seemed lost. Should we advance to scale the thicketed embankment, drawing enemy fire as we tried to ascend it? Should we retreat, recognizing that the Americans were not surprised, to regroup and attempt some other tactic? The only certainty was that we couldn't, shouldn't, remain where we were, in a meadow accepting enemy fire from higher ground.

At that moment Major Plenderleath appeared on horseback. "FitzGibbon! What's the best way to get at them?"

"The roadway, Sir. Where their artillery is placed."

"That's the way then. We'll wait until the firing of their cannon has finished. Reloading will take a half a minute, no more. We'll need to be quick."

The Frasier brothers, Alexander and Peter, two wild Scots who had been listening to Plenderleath, stepped forward. In his Scottish burr, Alexander, the elder of the two said, "We know what you have in mind, Major. Leave it to us. We'll lead the way."

"Assemble here." I shouted in a voice loud enough to be heard above our musket volleys, and strong enough to draw my company from the smoke and darkness.

Upon the artillery discharge, with the Frasiers in front screaming like demons loosed from hell, we rushed the cannon in some mad, ancient style—about forty of us. As soon as we could discern the colour of their jackets, bayonets were stuck into them. The gunners appeared unarmed and were easily done in, but the small detachment assigned to protect them put up a spirited defence. One bluecoat thrust his bayonet toward me. I parried it and brought my sword down where the shoulder meets the neck. His eyes widened in shock and terror at the finality of my blow. I was close enough to smell his breath. He fell to the side, the first man I'd ever killed. Another bluecoat charged me with bayonet extended. Quickly I stepped to the side, letting his momentum carry him. As he passed, with my right foot I pushed him with all my strength. He stumbled, falling on his face. Before he could rise I slashed him across the back. He screamed and tumbled forward again. My efforts did not compare with the Frasiers. I had never seen such savage ferocity; they battered their foe, dispatching them hastily so they could get to the next. An American grabbed the bridle of Major Plenderleath's horse, yelling 'Identify yourself'. The Major replied 'A friend' as he drew his pistol and shot him in the head, just before a volley of musket balls staggered his horse. Shrieking, the poor animal collapsed beneath him and the Major cursed in pain at some flesh wound. In the midst of this mayhem, Sergeant Frasier appeared pushing a stocky officer with the look of a blacksmith about him, back towards the British line. His dazed prisoner kept repeating himself, 'Where is the line? Where is the line?' The Sergeant had captured himself a general, judging by the gold epaulets. Off to the side, the younger Frasier had another officer pinned to the earth with his boot. This one had a map in hand and wore a dress uniform more suited for entertaining ladies at some evening soiree. He squirmed about, yelling "Stop this. Do you know who I am?" I heard Frasier reply, "Aye Sir, I do. You're the man who'll be dead in a minute if you don't keep still."

Not long after, American buglers sounded retreat. In less than an hour the battle was over. Orders came down for us to move back and conceal ourselves in the woods as Colonel Harvey did not want dawn's light to reveal how few of us there actually were.

It was difficult to be joyous. The battlefield became visible with the first light. The trampled, stained fields and the roadway on the far rim were littered with bodies, perhaps four hundred of them in jackets of red or blue, amidst the dead and dying horses and farmer's cows. Badges, buttons, bayonets, and other military accoutrements caught the early morning rays of the sun. My company was assigned the task of helping to clear the field. Moans and shallow calls for water alerted us to those most in need. Agonized men were carted to the surgeon's tent near Davis' Tavern. Quivering, wounded animals with panicked eyes were put out of their misery. Anything of value was removed from the dead-cartridge boxes, knapsacks, and boots still wearable. The bodies of British soldiers were taken to their final resting place in the cemetery by the little church. When the Americans didn't return under flag of truce to retrieve their dead, their corpses were buried in a mass grave on a knoll by the road near where the artillery had been. Spending the day wandering among the dead and barely living did much to harden my spirit.

What had been so near to disaster ended in brilliant victory. Capturing Generals Chandler and Winder and leaving their troops in uncertainty without orders proved to be the key. When tallies were taken, American losses totalled three hundred fifty, and a quarter of the brave men who marched from Burlington Heights were casualties. This war was proving itself to be much more than an adventure to me.

I would not allow myself to think of the men I'd killed. Someone had to die. That is the nature of war. If it hadn't been them, it would have been me.

# 23
## *Portage Road, June 1813*

Not long after Stoney Creek, Colonel Harvey summoned me
to his tent. It was situated beyond the towering shade trees
on Burlington Heights overlooking the calming blue waters
of the bay below. The flap on the tent was up to admit any
breeze wishing to find its way in. The Colonel was leaning
over a map spread out on a hastily assembled table. He looked
up as I entered, greeted me with a handshake and got to his
purpose directly.

"Ahh. FitzGibbon. Scouts tell me that the Americans have
retreated to the two forts they've captured. No doubt the
timely arrival of Commodore Yeo's little fleet hastened their
journey. However, our enemy has begun to torment the
people all along the Niagara. Foraging parties go into the
countryside and steal whatever food they can find. Some of
them are not averse to burning barns and crops when they're
done. This has to be stopped. That's your new assignment.
Stop the foraging. Intercept any communication between Fort
George and Fort Erie, and catch that damned traitor Joseph
Willcocks. The man is still a sitting member of the Legislative
Assembly! Sheaffe's replacement, General De Rottenburg, has
issued an arrest warrant charging him with treason."

"How will I do all this, Sir?"

"The army can spare twenty-five horses, no more. Choose fifty men from the 49th. Select whomever you want, just be sure they know enough about riding not to fall off the horses."

"I'll be needing a few things besides horses and men if we're to engage in these shadowy practices. We can't always be riding about in these bright red jackets. We'll need some settlers' clothes for disguise when it suits our purpose. And a few pistols. Can't always be using muskets on horseback while we're bouncing about."

"I'll instruct the Quartermaster to provide whatever you ask. Within reason of course."

"In the King's name we'll do some terrorizing of our own."

"That's the spirit. Leave as soon as possible once you've chosen your men. Any supplies that aren't ready when you depart I'll send to De Cew House. It's near Beaver Dams, not far from Twenty Mile Creek. Do you know it?"

"No, but we'll find it."

"Good man. Do harm to any American soldier that leaves those forts."

"Understood."

Within two days we were on our way. There weren't fifty men in the entire regiment who knew their way around a horse, but enough to instruct the others. This was an extraordinary assignment we'd been given and there was an air of excitement among the men. They'd even begun calling themselves "The Green-uns" referring to the colour of the facings on their redcoats.

I mapped out the Niagara and divided the men into small parties. From our base at Militia Captain John De Cew's farm we scoured the countryside. We travelled different tracks through woods and ravines, sometimes in red, sometimes not, whichever suited our purposes. When word reached us about marauders harassing an area we'd find the enemy and set an ambush for them. Skirmishing was a daily occurrence. If we could capture or kill the foragers, we did; if outnumbered we attempted some deception to frighten them away, often using Indian war cries. The aim was to convince anyone who left the security of the forts that their lives were in jeopardy. We accomplished this well enough; the citizens of Niagara began to refer to their protectors as "The Bloody Boys". The lads were proud of this name they'd been given.

The worst scavengers of the lot were freebooters from Buffalo led by one Doctor Cyrenius Chapin. Apparently Chapin saw war as an opportunity to improve his fortunes. He and his "Forty Thieves" as the locals called them, looted whomever they chose. They weren't just after food, but valuables that could be sold for profit. And alcohol. They showed no preferences for type of alcohol. Only very brave or foolish men would attempt to resist. Stories came to us. More than one man died trying to stop his possessions from being stolen. Chapin was said to find enjoyment in what he did. He seemed to be looking for any justification for murder. I desperately wanted to catch him.

Our game was one of cat and mouse, but some days it was difficult to tell who was the cat and who was the mouse. On one occasion Hennessy, Given, and I were travelling in a wooded region that skirted the Portage Road around the Falls. We were hunting couriers bringing messages between the two forts. As we were about to exit the trees and cross the roadway a band of riders, perhaps a dozen or so, each wearing at least some item of apparel in blue, rounded a turn in the road. At quick glance their leader had a waxed mustache and whiskers on his chin, the trademark of Chapin himself. Had he seen us? Seriously outnumbered, we darted into the interior of the wood. We scampered along paths made narrower by the lush summer growth. Branches slapped us as we passed. Outrunning the enemy would not be easy as our mounts were not fresh after a long morning's travel. Eventually we burst into a more forested space, with little undergrowth beneath the monstrous oaks and maples. We were more visible and sought some hiding place to conceal ourselves. No one dared look back. In an area layered with rocky ledges nearer the river, past a place natives might have used as a campsite, we found what we were after. Beneath a ledge hidden from view by luxuriant vines there was seclusion enough for three horses. We dismounted, calmed the horses and waited, hoping only to hear the cheerful chattering and singing of birds. Instead we heard the clattering and snorting of horses, the leathery sounds of men dismounting, and pursuers too close for comfort. Thoughts of indignities in a prison camp in Holland intruded my consciousness. More than the fear of dying, the shame of being taken prisoner unsettled me. But there were no angry commands. The men were jesting with one another. They seemed to have stopped to rest from the heat of the mid-day sun in the cool shade of these trees. Perhaps it was they who had been here before. Any noise from our animals would alert them to our presence. We soothed our mounts as best we could. Flies buzzing about annoyed the horses, who wanted to flick them off with their tails. Sweat trickled from our armpits. More and more it sounded as if these bandits were drinking: the volume of their jovial conversation went up and the laughter increased. The minutes dragged on. Our enemy gave no indication of departure. Waiting was too dangerous, so I signalled Hennessy and Given with my hands. I removed my pistol from its holster and drew my sword from its scabbard. They followed my lead, slinging muskets from their backs, loading them, and checking the pistols in their belts. Five shots in total before we'd need to reload.

"On command howl like banshees. Fire your first shot at the man in the mustache," I whispered.

We rushed from our hiding place making a grand imitation of ancient Gaelic spirits warning death. Half drunk Chapin's men were unable to make sense of what was happening. They threw their jugs in our direction and scattered. Three musket balls whizzed at Chapin. One must have nicked his arm because he yelped and shook his arm twice as though this might rid himself of the pain. Another ball hit a burly rider as he scurried to mount his horse. He fell back like a dead weight. The rest scampered off without looking back. As for us, not wanting to give our adversaries a chance to reconsider, we galloped off in the opposite direction.

A week later my luck held again. While the 'Bloody Boys' were occupying themselves removing the planks from the bridge over the Chippawa River in hopes of some future ambush, I rode off on Guard to scout the region beyond. Nailed to trees and fences, posters had begun to appear all along the Portage Road. Recruits were wanted for the Canadian Volunteers, a unit to be composed entirely of Upper Canadians willing to fight for the Americans under the command of Joseph Willcocks. Interested parties were instructed to join him at Fort George. Whenever I found one, I replaced it with one of my own, announcing who was 'Wanted for Treason.'

Where the Portage Road intersects Lundy's Lane sat Deffield's Tavern. Its owner had been a good friend to us. That day the horse of an American dragoon was tethered to a rail outside it. Thinking that this might belong to a courier stopping for a drink on a delightful June afternoon before continuing on his way with a message of some importance, I stopped. Perhaps this was a man who might share a few more secrets over a free drink from a fellow traveller. Composing my most good natured self I entered. I'd no sooner said, "That's a gorgeous horse out there! Would you be wanting to sell him? I'll trade mine and a handful of American dollars for that beauty," when the dragoon spun to face me and reached across himself with his right hand to unholster the pistol on his left. I rushed him and before he could extend his shooting arm in my direction I pushed it skyward with my left hand. With my right fist I thumped him in the kidneys, again and again in quick succession. He grimaced and grunted with each blow but would not release that pistol. Then the situation worsened. There was movement in the back of the darkened room. Another bluecoat bolted upright, knocking over the chair he'd been sitting upon. He raised his musket wanting to fire, but feared hitting the dragoon positioned between us. I made no effort to give him an easy shot and continued to punch my human shield. After seconds of frustration the bluecoat considered another possibility. He placed the musket on a table and detached the bayonet. He lifted it above his head like a hunter might a long knife to drive down into his quarry. The bluecoat planned to come up behind the dragoon and slam the bayonet down into my exposed shoulder. Deffield's missus, who had been doing something back of the bar, recognized his intent as well and rushed out, grasped his raised arm from behind with both of hers and pulled back with all her might. She fell to the floor. The bluecoat stumbled backwards. After shrugging her off, he kicked her feet out of his way and started forward. As hard as I could I kicked my dragoon on his right shin. When he buckled, I yanked his up stretched arm to the side and back and pulled the trigger of his pistol. There was an explosion inches from my attacker's chest. He stood motionless and disbelieving for an instant and dropped to the floor. To complete my task I slugged the dragoon on the jaw. Less than half a minute had passed. I helped my heroine from the floor, checking to see that she was not hurt. Then I hugged her in thanks for rescuing me.

The shot brought her husband running from outside. He scratched his head in bewilderment at what he saw: two American soldiers on the floor of his tavern, one bleeding all over it, and another man hugging his wife, perhaps too enthusiastically.

These incidents made entertaining stories to share with the lads at supper, but when terrifying images disturbed my sleep and I lay there alone, I'd wonder how long a man could dance with death and not fall.

# 24
## *Beaver Dams, June 1813*

Whenever there was a moment of peace, I would read and reread my treasured letters from Mary Haley. Propped up against an ancient oak on John De Cew's property I was considering how to reply to Mary's latest letter, how to put my true feelings for her into words, when my reflection was disturbed by the sight of two Mohawks escorting a delicate-looking woman toward me. The woman had removed her bonnet and carried it in her hand. Whatever had held her fine, dark hair in place had loosened, allowing strands to free themselves. The bottom of her skirt was muddied. The fabric was torn in one place. The stitching on her left shoe had split revealing a stained stocking. Her brown dress was dampened under the arms. Initially she looked quite fatigued, but became excited when she saw me.

Rising from my place on the grass, I inquired, "Mrs. Secord?" The woman was familiar to me. The Secords owned a store in Queenston. Her husband had suffered injury in battle at the Heights the previous year. We had met before. "How do you come to be here?"

"I'm so glad I've found you, Lieutenant FitzGibbon. I feared I'd never reach you in time. Avoiding the main roads so

I would not be detained by the Americans has lengthened my journey." She paused to catch her breath.

"You've come all the way from Queenston?"

"I left before sunrise. My husband urged me to go only as far as St. David's to relay the message to my step-brother. We thought he could bring it to you, but he was ill with fever. I continued on hoping that Captain Merritt might be at home. He was not. There was no one else. At times I felt I couldn't go on, but I knew I must. I thought I'd never survive the mosquitoes near Black Swamp. Eventually I stumbled upon the Indian encampment. They speak no English. Did you know that? I just kept repeating your name, 'FitzGibbon, FitzGibbon' and they brought me here. They behaved like perfect gentlemen."

"My God woman, the route from Queenston to DeCew by way of Black Swamp is nearly twenty miles. I'll be sure to provide you with refreshment, but first, what have you come to tell me?"

"I've come to warn you. The Americans have discovered you are quartered here with the DeCews. A small army will soon be on its way to finish off the Bloody Boys."

"How do you know this?"

"Last evening, two officers stopped at our home demanding food and lodging. We had no choice but to oblige. They ordered me to provide their meal. While I cooked they drank their whiskey and became boisterous. They chattered about their exploits to come and boasted about what they'd do to you and your men when they reached DeCew. The better part of a regiment will be leaving Fort George. I was only able to make out bits and pieces of what they said as I went about my chores. James heard everything. The musket ball in his knee still keeps him in bed."

"You're certain? This was not some deception."

"James is. He wouldn't have sent me otherwise. May God grant that no harm come to my family. My eldest daughter was to prepare breakfast for them. The younger ones were to look after the baby. If the officers noticed my absence, James was to offer some explanation that they might accept, about a neighbour needing a midwife."

"I'll not forget this bravery. Do not worry. The Americans will not suspect. We'll make preparations for their uninvited visit. I'm sure that Mrs. DeCew will find somewhere for you to rest after you've eaten. In the morning some of my men will take you home."

Two days subsequent to Mrs. Secord's warning, on June 24th, I watched the enemy approach with my telescope. They must have travelled throughout the night because the morning sun was just rising behind them in the eastern sky as they neared the marshy area about two miles from DeCew, known as Beaver Dams. Cavalry accompanied the infantry. Perhaps five hundred in all marched through the cornfields that separated the marshes from the edge of the escarpment. Little did they know that they were being stalked. Four hundred warriors watched them from the woods. There were two hundred Caughnawaga Mohawks from Montreal, with a few Mississaugas and Ojibways thrown in for good measure, under a fur trader named Dominique Ducharme, and two hundred Haudenosaunee from Grand River with William Kerr, still proud of his immaculate top hat. John Norton and the old chieftain's son, John Brant were present as well.

When the enemy column had advanced far enough along the road to be fully engulfed by the cornfield, the skirmishing began in earnest. The warriors had sniped at the Americans earlier as they travelled along, just to unnerve them, but now there was intensity to the action. Officers and cavalry men were especially vulnerable to their fire, sitting atop their horses, visible above the corn. Several went down right away, including the one I'd guess to be their commander. Eventually, they all dismounted to protect themselves. The Mohawks darted in and out the fields, shooting at any sign of blue. Those who left the column to pursue their attackers regretted that decision. Few returned. Skirmishing was greatest at the rear of the column to discourage any thought of retreat. Fleeing into the uncertainty of the marshes was daunting. That left only moving forward. To prevent this, the Bloody Boys had arranged a deception. To give the impression that there were more of us than there actually were, my redcoats moved in and out of the beech wood laced with evergreens, on the western edge of the cornfield. As intended, they were only partially hidden by the underbrush. The few of us with swords rode about letting the rays of the sun flash on our weapons at intervals, suggesting that British officers were present in force. Small parties of 'the Boys' dashed toward the enemy, hooting and hollering to attract attention, then raced back to the security of the forest. Our pantomime looked like a clumsy attempt to lure the enemy into the unknown. I gambled that these Americans knew that other armies had pursued too vigorously only to perish in ambush and would not take the bait. My estimation proved correct. Fear must have immobilized them. None had the stomach for hand-to-hand combat with an undetermined number of natives and British redcoats. The column just stayed where it was. Casualties slowly mounted.

About three hours after the skirmishing had begun, I decided to press our advantage. With a white handkerchief tied to my upraised sword I rode toward the Americans. Two captains came out to meet me.

"I'm Lieutenant James FitzGibbon of His Majesty's Army. I'm the spokesman for Lieutenant Colonel John Harvey. Who might you two be?"

The more prosperous of the two, judging by the quality of his uniform and the impressiveness of his horse, spoke first. "I'm Captain MacDowell of the United States Fourteenth Infantry." Gesturing in the direction of the other he added, "And this is Captain Hall of the Dragoons."

"Shouldn't I be communicating with a more superior officer?"

They exchanged irritated glances with one another before MacDowell replied, "We'll be sure to relay messages to Colonel Boerstler."

"Not sure if I should be 'parlez'ing with the likes of you. We're wantin' to know if you're ready to surrender. Do you two have the authority to answer a question like that?"

"Colonel Boerstler wants to know how many redcoats there are. Have them come out of the woods. He won't surrender to an unseen army."

"You won't be telling us to do anything! The only thing we'll be showing you is a murderous band of warriors removing tomahawks and scalping knives from their belts. Have not enough of your soldiers died? This little expedition of yours has failed. My question to you is simple enough: are you ready to surrender or will serious bloodshed be required?"

Hall replied, "We'll need to discuss this with our Colonel. We'll let you know by the end of the day."

"Wait until the end of the day! You're demented. Five minutes is all you've got to decide. You bloody well better surrender before I lose control of my allies. If that happens we'll both regret your dithering."

"Would we have your word as a British officer that no harm will come to anyone if we do as you say? United States soldiers will need to be treated respectfully, as prisoners of war. We'd expect that men will be allowed to keep their personal possessions. Militiamen must be paroled. Can you promise this?" asked MacDowell.

"Is that bandit Chapin with you?"

"He is, but our Colonel is insistent. Our terms as expressed are the minimum conditions."

Thinking of the greater good, and wishing to conclude negotiations before something unexpected altered circumstances. I agreed to their terms. They requested permission to get Boerstler's official consent to surrender. As they were about to depart I reminded them, "Five minutes, boys. No more. Or God help you."

As they were scurrying back, Major De Haven came up beside me. He had arrived with a small detachment that joined the 'Bloody Boys' hidden from view. As ranking officer he was now the one who should become the chief negotiator. Because he did not know all that had transpired, I feared the Major would give something away. I whispered, "With respect Sir, you mustn't utter a word. The Americans are about to become my prisoners. Not a word."

De Haven bristled at my insolence, but did as he was instructed. I knew tomorrow I'd receive a good dressing down.

When the two captains returned, MacDowell said only, "Colonel Boerstler will surrender his army on condition that you keep to his terms."

Things went as they should with one exception. No one was harmed, but the natives disregarded my instructions concerning personal property. They believed that possessions were the prizes of war. Horses, pistols, belts, and other valued items were all 'liberated' from their owners. There was nothing I could do to stop it.

After all of the enemy weapons were confiscated and the professional soldiers secured, the process of paroling the militiamen was begun. I saw to that myself. Thirty militiamen queued up in front of the little table where I sat with papers spread out. There was a strong sense of relief among them, knowing that they'd be heading home not bound for a prison ship in the St. Lawrence River off Quebec. The expectation of parole emboldened their leader, who stood first in line. He spoke to me in dismissive tone.

"Lieutenant FitzGibbon, I presume. Can we complete this process as quickly as possible?"

Without glancing up I replied, "Right you are, Doctor Chapin. I hoped that an opportunity to meet you might present itself." With great care I dipped the nib of my pen in the beautiful, silver-lidded glass jar that contained the ink, and offered it to him. "Do you know what you're promising when you place your signature on these papers, Doctor?"

He snatched the pen from my hand. "I know what I'm doing, man. Where do I sign?"

I indicated the spot. Bending over he noted his name with quite a flourish. When he straightened up I was no longer seated. Instead I was looking him directly in the eyes. With all the menace I could muster I replied, "I hope you do know what you're doing Chapin. Hate to think you won't be keeping your word. The war is over for you. If I ever hear that you're bothering anyone on this side of Niagara I'll personally come searching for you. When I find you, I'll kill you. Don't doubt that. It'll be a matter of honour. At the moment before you die you'll remember this little conversation. It'll be me keeping my word. Maybe I'll have the pleasure of watching you dangle from one of these grand Canadian trees with a noose around your neck. Maybe I'll be too far away to see the recognition in your eyes when my musket ball smashes into your skull, but you'll know who sent it. Do you comprehend what I'm telling you?"

Chapin sneered at me and practically hissed his reply. "Someday when we've won this war, FitzGibbon, I'll see to you."

My eyes did not leave his. Tapping his sleeve about the spot where our musket ball must have nicked him two weeks earlier near the Portage Road, I said, "If you are still alive."

Wincing at my touch, he looked away.

The rest of his men shuffled forward and gave me their names. I recorded them as best I could. They put an 'X' next to whatever I'd written.

When Lieutenant-Colonel Harvey completed his military report for submission, a number of things worthy of note were included. At Beaver Dams twenty-five officers, nearly five hundred soldiers including fifty mounted dragoons, and the colours of the U.S. Fourteenth Infantry were captured. Thirty mounted militiamen were paroled. Not a single cartridge had been fired by a British regular. The Caughnawaga Mohawks had done most of the fighting. The Haunosaunee Mohawks acquired most of the loot, and a certain Lieutenant had proven himself to have quite a way with words.

# 25
## *Black Rock, July 1813*

In the darkest part of the night we rowed across the mist-shrouded Niagara River bound for Black Rock on the American side. The men pulled hard on their oars so the current wouldn't cause the bateaux to drift downstream toward the Falls. Only the rhythmic sounds of the oars slipping in and out of the water broke the silence.

I was in the lead boat next to the organizer of the raid, Lieutenant-Colonel Cecil Bisshopp. He had assembled two hundred regulars from the 41st, the 8th,, the 'Bloody Boys', and forty Lincoln militiamen as well. Our objective was to ransack the supply depot in the little village a few miles outside the town of Buffalo and make off with whatever goods we could carry. It seemed a simple enough task.

Cecil Bisshopp had earned a reputation as an able and enterprising officer. He was thought to be a rising star in the British army. Less than thirty years of age, he was already a Lieutenant-Colonel. Money alone couldn't purchase promotions that quickly. He was well-liked by the men who served under him. He treated them all as comrades-in-arms. Social class did not separate them. The extra ration of rum that he'd ordered for his soldiers earlier in the week only enhanced his popularity. Since meeting him in late May I had gotten to know this fellow officer. He was a grand lad, an amiable companion, and irrepressibly cheerful. As a soldier he was deliberate, purposeful, and reliable.

"Nothing like a good mist to set the mood and heighten the senses, eh Fitz?" he whispered in my ear.

"Voices carry on the water, Colonel. Might be safer if nothing was said," I replied in my softest voice.

"If the creaking of the oars in their sockets doesn't alert them, neither will a little whispering. Have you heard the splendid news from Europe?"

"No."

"One of Napoleon's Grand Armies has been crushed by the Russians. Never imagined that the French would be foolish enough to try to reach Moscow before the winter set in. No one can survive a bloody Russian winter."

Whether Bisshopp chattered away to prevent anxiety from waylaying him, or because he had no nerves at all, I do not know, but he was certainly intent upon a monologue. "I'm told that your Canadian winters are nearly as bad. Should be a bracing experience. Snowshoeing sounds great fun. Napoleon's Russian campaign must have cost him more than a few men. Should make things easier for the Iron Duke in Spain. Don't you agree?"

"Yes Sir. You saw action in Europe with Wellington?"

"Holland, Portugal, Spain—all the spots an English traveller would want to see. I must admit the tranquillity of the English countryside beckoned me now and then." Chuckling to himself he continued, "Actually it was my father who did most of the beckoning. Wants me home to look after the estate and manage family affairs. Only son and all that. Not ready to play the gentleman yet. I've endeavoured to explain to him the beauty of midnight river cruises like this, but I've failed to sway him. Can you see me as a country squire, Fitz? How would I fill my days?" He was quiet for a few minutes, as if he was considering the questions he posed for himself. Then he commenced again. "Poetry. That's it. I'll become a poet. Should impress the ladies, eh Fitz. Do you read it yourself?"

As he seemed to expect an answer, I replied, "Not much opportunity to do so."

"Ahh. When this little errand of ours is finished, we'll remedy that. I've written a few poems myself. We'll split a few bottles of claret and I'll read you some. Even my words will appear to have merit after a little refreshment."

It was not long before we reached the American shore; the river is less than a mile across there. Bisshopp was the first to jump onto the pebbled beach. With calm authority and gestures he directed the men as though this were some parade ground exercise conducted dozens of times. "Hurry boys. We need to be back home for breakfast. I'm feeling peckish already."

No sentries sounded alarm. No one was waiting to repel our assault. Clearly we were not expected. After we'd surrounded the barracks, a grinning Bisshopp waved me forward. "Let's hear what you can do."

Understanding what he wanted, I called out loudly, "Who's in charge here? Representatives of His Majesty the King wish to know."

Following a commotion within the barracks, sleepy militiamen in night shirts tumbled out the doors holding unloaded muskets. They froze when they saw double rows of redcoats holding muskets aimed at them. A bootless young man, still tucking his shirt into his pants, rushed to the front. At a guess he was the son of whomever was purchasing muskets and supplies for this little band of volunteers.

"The British army demands the immediate surrender of this post. Are you the man I'd be speaking to about that?"

He nodded.

"You're the ranking officer here, lad?"

Uncomfortably he nodded again. The American militia-men behind him clustered around him, not wanting to miss a word.

"Colonel Bisshopp has instructed me to offer you the safety of surrender and parole. He feels no need to kill husbands, fathers, and sons of innocent families unless you oblige him to do so. Consider his offer carefully. Should you refuse, you're mere seconds away from a welcome to the afterlife. If you're sure you're bound for heaven, take your chances. Otherwise throw down your weapons."

Behind the officer there was noise. Muskets thudded on earth. Then there was movement. The citizen soldiers were slipping away into the night. The officer turned to watch them go, at first a few, then the rest. He made no effort to do any-thing about it.

I chided him. "Sir, this is most irregular. Your men are quit-ting the field before we have agreed to terms."

Shamefacedly he replied, "I know, but I can not stop them."

"I see it, Sir. I will not detain you. You may retire as well." With relief showing on his face, he made some attempt at a bow and scurried off. In the moonlight, which had just found its way through the clouded sky, we observed the militiamen running downhill towards Buffalo. They had just learned an important lesson: war is much more than spectacle.

Bisshopp emerged from behind me. "Well done, Lieutenant. Remind me never to play cards with you. You'd manoeuvre me as you wished and I'd lose the family fortune." Then raising his voice he shouted, "Hurry up men. Carry out your assignments. Take whatever is worth having. Fill the bateaux and the scow in the dockyards that our friends have been kind enough to leave for us. Then fill our own boats. Those militiamen are running fast enough to be in Buffalo in twenty minutes. We don't wish to make the acquaintance of any more Americans tonight."

We went about our business. We confiscated three small cannon and spiked the larger pieces so they could not be fired. Lines were formed to pass canister and round shot along, to get it into the boats quickly. Sacks of powder were carried. Crates of musket cartridges were dragged. Whatever military stores we could find in their warehouses were grabbed. Bisshopp sent the American bateaux off as soon as they were loaded. A cache of salt was discovered. The soldiers who hadn't left rolled the barrels to the remaining boats, while 'The Boys' set fire to the empty barracks, the blockhouse, the storehouses, and the schooner in their dockyards. It was unfortunate that we had to destroy the schooner, but none of us were sailors. Moving the barrels took longer than anticipated; there were one hundred eighty in all. To this point nothing had disturbed us. Then single shots rang out. From the shore militiamen newly arrived could be seen in the light from the flames that by now were consuming all of the buildings in Black Rock. They were moving into firing positions.

I ran to the Colonel. "Sir, let's abandon the salt. The few barrels we've loaded will be enough."

"The army cooks will not thank us if we leave this prize behind." Then he shouted to those doing the heavy lifting. "Put your backs into it men. A few more barrels and we'll depart. We'll miss breakfast if we don't leave soon."

"Bisshopp, we've suffered no casualties. We should leave now."

"Soon."

The enemy musket fire was no longer sporadic; the intensity increased. The skirmishers became bolder, moving forward for better shots. Redcoats began to fall.

"Sir!" I screamed.

Bisshopp finally acquiesced. "To the boats!"

Abandoning anything still on the beach we scrambled into the boats. A musket ball pierced the Colonel's left thigh as he was climbing aboard. The oarsmen pulled with all their strength. Balls raked our bateau again. Another two suffered. Before we had gone any great distance a ball smashed Bisshopp's left wrist; another nicked his right arm.

"Are you all right, Sir?" I asked, but seeing the pain in his face it was easy to tell he wasn't. He clenched his jaw to keep from crying out. When he saw me looking down at his shattered wrist, he whispered, "Nothing to worry about, Fitz. I'm right-handed. Shouldn't interfere with my career as a poet."

"Never thought it would," I replied as we were rowed out of range.

The objective of our mission was achieved. We'd stolen valued supplies from the Americans and diminished their ability to fight. We'd added to our own military stores and sent a message that it was going to be a long war unless they discontinued their hostilities. But at what cost? Fifteen of our number were killed or wounded. If only we had departed sooner.

Five days later, I received word that Cecil Bisshopp, a man of gentle and generous nature, had succumbed to his injuries and died.

# 26
## *Crysler's Farm, November 1813*

In early October the *Buffalo Gazette* proclaimed it. Our spies provided confirmation. They were gone; the American regiments that had been assembling near Buffalo, for what we anticipated would be another invasion of Niagara, had marched along the river, been loaded onto a flotilla of small craft, and embarked across Lake Ontario. That could only mean one thing: an assault on Kingston or even Montreal was imminent. The only wonder was why they hadn't attempted it sooner.

The 49th was ordered to set off after them. Along dampened roadways, through fields of grasses heavy with dew, we marched briskly to the lively, fife tunes played by drummer boys. The splendour of the Canadian autumn, with the vibrant colours of the maple, oak, and sycamore—crimson, gold and orange—kept our spirits high, at least at the start.

No sooner had we departed on bateaux from near Head-of-the-Lake than a fierce storm overtook our convoy. Gale force winds assailed us. The single sails of our boats had to be lowered to prevent us from being blown further from shore and tipping over. Waves rose up in angry protest of the westerly wind and attempted to wrench control from the anxious oarsmen. Rain pelted down. I was nauseous and as usual knew that my stomach would do whatever it wished. I feared for my life and considered how entirely unsuitable it would be for a soldier's life to end in drowning. Fortunately, the oarsmen managed to get us to the safety of York harbour before the worst of the storm's wrath. Nature held us prisoner for days. Our sole consolation was that the winds must have battered the Americans as well, holding them up in the little inlets and rivers on the lake's southern shore, giving them no added advantage.

When the storm abated and conditions improved we set off again for Kingston. We took turns at the oars. Men rowed until muscles ached, cramped, and were of no use.

One chill morning as we glided through the melancholy mist released by the warmer lake waters, Kingston came into view. I could imagine an artist with few colours on his palette wanting to paint this scene. The formidable charcoal fortress on the hill above the harbour stood in silhouette against a bank of grey clouds sitting on the horizon beneath a paler grey sky. The setting matched our mood. Cold, wet, and cheerless we'd arrived at our destination.

That evening we officers of the 49th gathered in front of the roaring fire in our mess beneath a candled chandelier, warming our hands with mugs of heated rum. We congratulated one another on escaping a watery death. The company was most amiable: the decisive John Harvey, the daring Charles Plenderleath recently recovered from his wounds suffered at Stoney Creek, and another fifteen experienced soldiers who understood what the army required. The good natured conversation ceased when two gentlemen in uniform entered the room. The first was a distinguished, silver-haired officer. By the deference he was being shown I guessed him to be Major General De Rottenberg, Sheaffe's replacement, the man who'd written the manual on skirmishing Isaac Brock had seen me reading a decade ago. If I remembered correctly his wife was said to be the most beautiful woman in

Montreal. Trailing behind De Rottenburg was a young, thin-faced man, ramrod-stiff in his deportment and most precise in his movements. This proved to be Lieutenant-Colonel Joseph Morrison, commander of the 89th Regiment, fresh from Spain. De Rottenburg approached Lieutenant- Colonel Harvey and addressed him in words tinged with a German accent. The rest of us were permitted to listen in.

"I have news to share with you. Regrettably, there is more bad than good. The Royal Navy positioned on Lake Erie under the command of Admiral Barclay has been defeated at Put-in-Bay. The Americans now control that lake. This placed Colonel Proctor in an untenable situation. Fearing encircle-ment, he was forced to abandon Amherstberg. He attempted a stand against General Harrison inland, near the village of Moraviantown. He was unsuccessful. The remains of his army has fled to Burlington Heights. Tecumseh is dead and our native allies are scattered. Our entire western defence has collapsed."

Complete silence filled the room as each of us considered the implications of the General's words. He continued. "Now the Northern Army of the United States, seven thousand strong, has collected on Grenadier Island, not far from here, where the waters of Ontario flow into the St. Lawrence River. The American target is yet unknown. Perhaps this is it. Perhaps it will be Montreal. The 49th will ready itself for both eventu-alities. Should the enemy head down river to Montreal, you will set off after them without delay. Are there any questions, Lieutenant- Colonel Harvey?"

"You will inform me if and when we are to depart?"

"Lieutenant-Colonel Morrison will instruct you. He is senior and will have overall command of such an expedition. Officers of the 49th, do not be discouraged. Although the situation is dire, not all news is troublesome. At Chateauguay, south of Montreal, an American incursion has been turned back by

Charles de Salaberry and his Voltigeurs Canadiens. Valour such as this is all that I require of you. Do not disappoint me."

With that De Rottenberg left us. As Morrison passed he whispered in my ear. "The General wishes to speak with you in the hall." I turned and followed, quickly trying to calculate what this might be about.

De Rottenberg wasn't frowning—a good sign. "Lieutenant FitzGibbon, it is good to meet you at last. Your name appears often in the reports I receive. Credit is due."

"Thank you, General. It is an honour and a pleasure to meet you."

"A captaincy is coming available. It is with the Glengarry Light Fencibles. Do you know of them?"

"Yes, Sir. Local lads, recruited to the King's service in North America for the duration of the war. Good at skirmishing I've heard."

"I'm offering you this promotion. It would begin New Year's Day. You would join them at Kingston. Do you wish it?"

It took less than an instant to decide. Better pay. Funds to reduce my accumulating debt. An opportunity to winter in Kingston where Mary Haley resided. "Yes. Thank you, Sir."

The General gave me a polite smile, and then with a nod in Morrison's direction, left. For weeks thereafter there was no movement from Grenadier Island. The only certainty was that chill winds were blowing the dying leaves from the increasingly barren trees. Winter was hovering nearby. Before the end of October snow fell for the first time, blanketing everything in white for a day or two before it melted. There was much speculation and wagering in the barracks about the enemy's intent. Whether conditions were forcing the Americans to reconsider their plans, or they were unable to decide upon their destination, I do not know. Each day of delay made an attack seem less likely. Only a mad man would begin a campaign on the brink of a Canadian winter with a army still in summer uniforms. Surely someone would remember the American defeat in a snowstorm at Quebec during the Revolutionary War. Someone must have heard of Napoleon's disastrous winter campaign to Moscow. Yet apparently no one had! In early November, on a day well-lit if not warmed by the sun, the Northern Army of the United States of America launched itself in small craft down the St. Lawrence, commencing the one hundred fifty mile journey through the five sets of rapids that would take them to Montreal.

Bewildered but determined to catch them, our own little army followed, first in bateaux, then on foot, comforted by the grey greatcoats, winter boots, and woolen fingerless gloves. It would have been difficult to keep pace with them, if the Americans hadn't taken extra time and preparation for their descent through the turbulent, rocky sections of the river. Navigating Gallop Rapids and Rapide du Plat proved no obstacle to us as our pilots were most familiar with them. The little villages of Upper Canada, Elizabethtown, Prescott, and Johnstown seemed empty, but on the American side, Morrisville, Ogdensburg, and Red Mills seemed hives of activity. Deserters informed us that every dwelling was crammed with the sick. Dysentery, the soldiers' disease, was inactivating men at an accelerating rate. Influenza, fever, and pneumonia were taking a toll as well. We heard that the sick were just being dumped on the doorsteps of their fellow citizens, without provision or arrangement for care, to die or heal themselves as the Almighty wished.

For safety, before the treacherous descent of the eight mile rapids known as Long Sault, the American army disembarked and marched on Canadian soil so only a few would remain in the boats to face the perils of the rapids. It was at this point that we began our skirmishing to annoy them. Our activity reminded me of a small dog in pursuit of a much larger one. We'd bark furiously at the behind of the larger dog until it turned and readied itself for reply. Then we'd scamper off, only to return once it resumed its forward movement.

On November 10 we camped for the night on a well-established farm. The distinctive, two-storey, cut-timber house was painted bright yellow and faced the King's Highway about one hundred feet from the river. Its numerous outbuildings suited our purposes. Much to my surprise I was acquainted with the owner from my time in York with General Brock. John Crysler was an elected member of the Legislative Assembly. Not only did he own this prosperous farm, but lumber concerns, mills, and other businesses as well. He was a sombre, taciturn man; I'd never seen him smile. Grumpily he watched us attend to our duties. I thought he looked very much like a man who expected battles to be fought on someone else's property and was about to be disappointed.

Later, I saw John Harvey standing near the open door of a gigantic barn, staring off into the darkness, so I approached him.

"What's more worrisome: the thought of catching them or not catching them?"

Harvey laughed. "Morrison's just asked me the same question. De Rottenberg has sent orders for us to break off engagement and return to Kingston. Morrison does not wish to do so, not when we're this close. He's asked for my support. I've given it. This had better go well or neither of us will have a command when this is done."

"Brock would be proud of the pair of you."

"Perhaps he would," replied Harvey. "Sickness has reduced their number. Some bluecoats have been sent ahead to Cornwall, but those who remain will outnumber us at least three to one. We'd better be up to the challenge."

The next day, November 11, Morrison set his twelve hundred men in formation on Crysler's farm, centred on Nine-Mile Road. It was a good position to defend. To the left was a swampy, pine forest fringed with rail fences keeping the wilderness at bay. Native warriors and militiamen were stationed within to keep us from being outflanked. To the right, about a half- mile from the forest, was the St. Lawrence River with five British gunboats anchored to prevent us from being outflanked on the right. Light companies of the 89th were hidden in the gullies containing streams that emptied into the river. In the middle, overlooking the black muck of drenched, furrowed fields that stretched for nearly a mile to the east, were the bulk of his troops, the 89th to the left, and the 49th to the right. The 89th, fresh from sunny Spain, removed their winter attire, choosing to fight as they were accustomed to with redcoats visible. The 49th saw no reason to chill itself.

An hour or two after mid-day, the Americans came out of the woods to the east in column formation in a most gallant style. The big dog couldn't ignore the challenge any longer.

The white, glistening frost that coated bushes and tree branches and covered the ploughed fields had finally disappeared when the battle began. Judging by the skirmishing sounds from the pine wood to our left, the opening American manoeuvre was to be an attempt at flanking our line to the left. Upon command the 89th, as no doubt they had been tirelessly drilled, turned precisely until they were at a forty-five degree angle to repulse whoever ventured from the pines. Before much thought could be given to this, British artillery appeared on our right. Two teams of horses pulling grey painted limbers with six-pound cannon attached clattered up next to us. The gunners scampered down from the horses and their seats on the limbers and hastily began their preparations. Guns were unhooked and positioned. Limber boxes were opened for access to the ammunition. Horses were withdrawn back to where waggons with extra supplies were waiting. The cannon were carefully elevated and primed for firing. One of the gunners placed a canister he planned to load on the ground, cut the fuse that protruded, and lit it. Then he placed it quickly in the barrel for another gunner to push it down with his ramrod, onto the bag of powder already there, pierced by a brass wire poked down the vent. A third artilleryman at the back lit the fuse for the cannon itself. With six foot recoil, the gun spat out the canister. Their calculations must have been correct. The bag of musket balls exploded just above the tightly packed columns of bluecoats, raining shrapnel down upon them. The two guns fired in tandem, perhaps a minute apart, for some time. It was a fearsome spectacle to see. The bluecoats stood still, awaiting their orders, and suffered dreadfully.

When the American infantry finally did move from columns into lines to advance across the muddied fields, they did not do so smoothly. Nothing was done in tight formation. It appeared that they had not drilled sufficiently, and perhaps, as was rumoured, the different regiments were not using the same drill manuals and the commands were confusing. As they moved forward, the lines became ragged. Companies would stop and fire when they wished, usually at a distance too great to cause much damage. When the American artillery commenced firing, that was a different matter. Luckily in the beginning their aim was too high and the round shot passed above our heads with the sound of rushing wind. When the artillerymen adjusted the elevations their aim improved. Cannon balls bounced in front of us, tearing into our lines with such speed that men in neither the front nor back rows could avoid them. Not far from me one of my company crumpled. I could not tell who was hit for his head was gone. Another man lay on the ground in shock trying to make sense of the bloody, jagged hole where his middle had been. I ignored a third as he plunged screaming to the side, no longer able to stand without his missing leg, and tried not to see another attempt to staunch blood flow with his hand from a shoulder that had once held an arm.

The true enemy in battle is fear. It devours self-assurance; it eats away at resolve; it saps strength, blurs vision and numbs the mind. If it takes hold all is lost. To calm my company I walked the line showing the composure that was required in the circumstance. There was no point in wondering how many of the enemy were targeting officers first, or considering the sporadic wasp-like buzzing about me.

"Lads, remember Detroit and Queenston Heights. Remember Stoney Creek and Beaver Dams. You're better soldiers than that lot. They can't even dress properly for winter! They'll be no dying today. None of you have my permission. You'll not want to face my wrath. Steady lads, steady. Hold your fire. We'll greet them all at once."

With bayonets affixed and muskets lowered, the bluecoats came forward to the steady beat of their drums. When they were about sixty paces away, our officers barked out the same command, "Make ready." The soldiers of the 49th thumbed the lock to full cock.

"Present.... First line, fire!" Half the regiment delivered a concentrated volley, fairly accurate at this distance. It staggered their front line. They stopped and raised their weapons to reply just as the second order was heard. "Second line, fire!" Spaces could be seen in their rows. The American momentum was lost, but they attempted to punish us with their gunfire. Both sides stood their ground, firing volley after volley of lead at the other. The gunfire was constant. We switched to fire by section, instead of entire row, to effect the sound of rolling thunder. White smoke flecked with unburnt powder hung above us, then blew slowly towards them, reducing our sight. No matter, lead would catch someone. Drummer boys scuttled about with upturned shakos filled with more cartridges, passing them to whomever needed them. For fifteen minutes the duel was sustained. Redcoat shoulders ached from the recoil, cheeks bruised, mouths dribbled black from where the teeth tore open the powder cartridges, perspiration glistened on faces despite the cold, and hands stung to the touch of heated metal.

Eventually the bluecoats could stand no more. We had fired three shots a minute to their two. Those who were left standing turned and hurled themselves through the lines of reinforcements coming up behind, unnerving them, breaking the will of the newcomers to proceed. They fled as well. Only the wounded, in pain and despair, and those who would never utter another word, remained on the field before us.

Of their own accord my lads lowered their muskets, waved their shakos above their heads and cheered in wild exaltation. On the far right by the river, clouds of smoke and musket fire could still be seen and heard, but the light companies of the 89th were well-positioned in the gullies and would be difficult to remove. Things looked most optimistic. Then the cheering stopped. On the far side of Crysler's field an American cavalry unit was assembling. They were forming themselves into two long lines, one behind the other, with about seventy-five per line. Even in the dull light their appearance was most impressive. Shiny buttons on their dark blue jackets, silver plates on their black helmets with shoulder-length white plumes dangling behind, and knee-length black leather boots contrasting with the white breeches were all visible, even at this distance. Their horses pranced, snorted, and bobbed their heads, anticipating their next command. The presence of dragoons was most unsettling. This was Upper Canada, not some grand Napoleonic battlefield. The 49th was still in line. We had expected no cavalry and practised no manoeuvre to repel their charge. Should the horsemen punch holes in our line and fight from behind us atop their mounts, or frighten the lads into running, they would hack us to pieces. To a man we knew that they must not be allowed to rout us.

In unison, the dragoons drew sabres from the scabbards on their left. The metallic sound they would make was easily imagined. They began their slow advance. The walk of the horses became a trot.

Hurriedly, redcoats unable to stand were pulled from where they lay so that the lines could be tightened and made more difficult to penetrate. Up and down the lines British commands rang out again. "Steady. Fix bayonets. Wait for the order."

I strode behind my men, reassuring them. "Wait for it lads. Now the fun begins. There'll be no retreat. We'll send the buggers to hell, or back the way they've come, whichever they'd prefer."

About a hundred yards out, the dragoons lowered their swords, pointing them in our direction. They spurred their animals to full gallop, at least as much of a gallop as the sloppy, uneven furrowed fields would allow. It was a fearful sight.

About thirty yards out, when we could clearly see the heaving chests and moist breath of their mounts, we fired. Horses shrieked. Horrified riders tumbled forward. Dragoons swerved to avoid colliding with the fallen. We fired again. The second blast staggered them. The charge faltered. The bluecoats had no stomach for the bayonets now raised against them to pierce their animals' chests and bring both beast and rider to the ground. There was to be no glorious triumph. They veered to the right, galloping off in disarray, leaving thirty dead and dying soldiers and beasts strewn in front of us.

As most of us were watching the cavalry depart, and the American infantry disappear into the woods on the eastern end of the field, from the corner of my eye I saw a redcoat leave his position in line to approach an injured dragoon who lay sprawled on the ground. The bluecoat raised his arm. I could almost hear his pleas for mercy. The soldier bayoneted him. No one said a word.

Once Colonel Harvey was reassured that the Americans were in full retreat, he summoned the officers of the 49th to begin the process of tallying our loses and assigning new duties. Counting himself, only seven of the eighteen officers who'd listened to General De Rottenberg in Kingston a few weeks past were present. The others were either wounded or dead. Major Plenderleath had received another thigh wound, but it was said was that there'd be no need to remove the leg. To my relief Harvey assigned some company other than mine to clear the battlefield. In my dreams I could still hear the anguished cries and moans from the wounded at Stoney Creek and had no wish for more memories. But he did have one special request.

"FitzGibbon, the officers that died today must be buried here in Upper Canada. Before that happens, cut off a lock of their hair to be sent home to the families. The hair will confirm what their loved ones do not wish to believe. It may serve as a memento. Perhaps it will provide some comfort. Can you see to that?"

I gaped at my commanding officer. What could I do, except assure him that it would be done? That night, beneath a shroud of darkness, I wandered with lantern in hand amidst the stretcher bearers spattered with red, and the blood drenched corpses, completing my sorrowful task.

In the days that followed, the results of the battle became known in more detail. Seven hundred bluecoats had been killed, wounded, or captured. Nearly two hundred redcoats under Morrison's command were no longer present for duty. The American army under General Wilkinson was vanquished. They had descended the rapids at Long Sault, and the abandoned all intent of reaching Montreal. It was reported that the bluecoats had crossed onto American soil and gone to ground for the winter in some lumber camp deep in New York State, except for the officers who were observed departing for the comfort of their own homes.

Upper Canada appeared to have survived another year, but there was plenty of war to come. As we journeyed back to our winter quarters in Kingston, there was much to consider.

# 27
# Kingston, December 1813

Snowflakes floated down from the starlit sky landing on the brim of my shako and the shoulders of my greatcoat. They found their way into my footprints in the earth's white covering. Nearly a year had passed since I'd last seen the Loyalist. There was never a more welcoming sight. Greyish-white smoke lazily eased itself from the red brick chimneys. Glow from the flickering candlelight in the front windows drew me forward. The cedar boughs on the cheerfully painted red door reminded me it was Christmas eve.

Entering the coach inn, I stood in the small foyer savouring its warmth and the sound of lively conversation emanating from the tavern room until William Haley noticed me. He approached, greeting me in jovial manner as was his custom. A young dog, of the type I had often seen working herds with its owner, tagged behind frantically wagging its tail, unable to contain heartfelt enthusiasm. "Welcome good sir. I'm glad that you are able to join us. It is always a pleasure to be of service to one of the King's men."

I slung my knapsack from my shoulder onto the floor, and William assisted me with the removal of my greatcoat, enquiring if I required a room, not really looking at my face. It was only when the hat pulled so low that it hid some of my features was removed that he recognized me. "James, is it you? How good to see you again. Should we have been expecting you? Mary said nothing."

"Mary doesn't know. Just yesterday the powers that be saw fit to grant some of us leave." Hearing more laughter from the bar room I added, "Your friends are in good spirits."

"Enjoying the spirit of the season they are. You'll stay with us, James. What an unexpected blessing it will be having you with us at Christmas!" As William placed my coat on one of the pegs on the wall, he took full notice of my newly tailored, yet to be paid for, forest green jacket and breeches. "You've no redcoat?"

"I've transferred from the 49th. Accepted a position as captain with the Glengarries."

"A promotion. Congratulations. Well-deserved. Why the green colour?"

"We're dressed like Wellington's 95th Rifles to intimidate the Americans, supposing they've ever heard of the 95th. Might work, at least until they discover we don't have any bloody rifles."

"A good regiment to be with?"

"It seems so. I've just begun to get to know the lads. Canadians most of them. Mainly of Scots descent. They've been telling me that their fathers served the King in some Highland regiment until they settled here. This bunch won't be letting anyone take away their farms. I'm sure I'll know a few more Gaelic oaths before long."

Chuckling to himself William replied, "A man can always benefit from knowing a variety of oaths suitable for all occasions." Then in more serious tone he said, "I trust you are in good health. You look it. Mary never reveals what's in those letters of yours. Once a week she travels further into town in search of them. Just by watching her return I can tell if the trip was successful. When your letters do arrive they come in a great bundle. Then she'll disappear for an hour. Perhaps I should stop prattling on. Go find her. She's in the kitchen."

As I headed into the dining room en route to the kitchen, from behind I could hear William's final comment. "That was such a shame about Newark."

I couldn't help myself. Slowly I returned to hear the news. "What was shameful?"

"The Americans burnt the entire town two weeks ago. We've just found out. People have been speaking about little else. It's terrifying. The men were all away serving with the militias. The women and children were given less than four hours to abandon their homes, taking what they could carry in the snow and freezing cold. T'was an evil thing to do."

"The enemy did such a thing?"

"A traitor ordered it. People recognized him. He used to represent them in the Legislature. He sat astride his horse and watched the flames devour everything. Joseph Willcocks. Do you know him?"

"Aye. Someone will need to make him pay for that." Truth be told, the last thing I wished to consider was the suffering of innocents, the requirements of justice, or the hatred stirring in my chest. "He will be held to account."

Reassured that justice would be done, William placed a fatherly hand upon my shoulder. "Stay with us as long as you wish, James."

"Thank you for your hospitality." Seeking respite from thoughts of war, I went off to the kitchen.

I stood in the kitchen doorway listening to the rustle of her skirt and watching her movement in the gentle light of the oil lamp that illuminated the room. From behind I could see the curves in the light brown fabric of the dress, the white bow made by the apron ties, and the red ribbon that held back her luxurious hair. She was preparing pies for the morrow's meal, so intent upon her task that she took no notice of me. It was comforting to observe her in the simplicity of daily life.

Eventually I enquired, "Miss, would you know where a good man can find sanctuary?"

She must have recognized my voice because she did not start at the unexpectedness of the question and responded with such composure. "For a good man there'd be a place in our family's pew at church. We'll be leaving for the Christmas Eve service soon. A man could find sanctuary there."

"That'll have to do if you can think of nowhere else." Mary turned and rushed to my arms. Letting them wrap around her she tucked herself into my chest. I could feel every breath. When I released her we gazed at one another. Mary Haley was more beautiful than I'd remembered. Even on the dampest night I hadn't imagined a woman as lovely as this. Seeing some herb hanging on the wall near the doorway I asked, "Is that mistletoe there on the wall?" Exaggerating my accent I added, "In this country is there any custom observed?"

Perplexed she replied, "That's not...," then changed tack. "What an observant man you are James FitzGibbon. Of course it is. And we Canadians cherish such customs." Mary leaned into me and kissed me, first with tenderness, later with more passion than I had ever known. Gently she grasped my face in her hands. "I knew you must be at Crysler's Farm. I was so afraid for you. The entire community lived in dread. News of the victory gave such relief. Thank God for success and your safety."

"The lads did well, but no more talk of war. I have a gift for you. Wait here." Retrieving my knapsack I withdrew a small glass jar with a silver lid, identical to the one I possessed myself. She fondled it with both hands when it was presented. "To store your ink. May it help you to remember me when you write."

"Your presence alone is greater gift than I could hope for." After kissing me again Mary went to the hutch in the dining room holding the inn's dishes, and from the drawer withdrew a package of paper held together by another red ribbon. For me.

Moved by her thoughtfulness, I still could not resist the opportunity to tease her. "What wonderful writing paper. The army will be impressed if I send my reports on paper such as this."

Frowning, Mary gently tapped my chest with the package. "If your general requires letters from you, let him provide his own paper!"

Smiling, I replied, "Of course. How callous of me. I shall use this paper for letters to you and no one else." And I kissed her.

During the next four months while my regiment wintered at Kingston, I was fortunate to spend many more off-duty hours at the Loyalist.

# 28
## *Oswego, May 1814*

Spring ushered in another season of war in Upper Canada. Throughout the winter I had prepared my company of Glengarries as best I could. Whenever weather conditions permitted, and often when they didn't, we practised the skirmishing skills that would be required of us when hostilities recommenced. News had come from Niagara that in retaliation for the burning of Newark, British forces had crossed the river, captured the American fort, and set ablaze every village between Lewiston and Buffalo. It was most disquieting that such a course of action had been taken. But there was no point in considering the necessity of inflicting such suffering on the innocent; the deed was already done. Retribution was inevitable. Conflict on the Niagara would surely intensify, and I fully expected my company to be ordered from Kingston with a moment's notice. However, this was not the assignment we were given.

Lieutenant General Gordon Drummond had been appointed the new commander of the British and Canadian forces in the upper province succeeding De Rottenburg. He had selected the intrepid John Harvey as his chief adjutant. It was Harvey that had come to explain the nature of the operation and my Glengarries' role in it. Drummond and

Commodore James Yeo of the Royal Navy stationed on Lake Ontario intended to raid Fort Oswego, the major American supply depot on the southern side of the lake. The primary objective was to seize cannon said to be bound for the newly constructed ships in the Sackets Harbour dockyards. According to Harvey, military materiel and supplies were brought up the Hudson River from New York City, ferried along the Mohawk River and across Lake Oneida, and transported down the Oswego River to the town protected by the fort. From the town goods were moved about forty miles on Lake Ontario to its south-east corner where the fortified naval base of Sackets Harbour with the deeper water, much preferred by the United States Navy, was located. The assault on Oswego was to be massive and my company was to take part.

As soon as the ice that hemmed the Royal Navy into Kingston harbour melted we set off. I thought our little fleet most impressive. There were eight warships in all. The two largest, HMS *Prince Regent* and HMS *Princess Charlotte* carried more than fifty cannon apiece. The remaining vessels were almost as intimidating: the sloops held about twenty guns each, and the brigs at least fourteen. Smaller gunboats followed in our wake. Our miniature armada bore over a thousand marines, sailors, and soldiers. There was much to observe on our ship during the journey. Sails flapped rhythmically in the breeze. Nimble sailors scampered about in rigging high above deck. Invigorating spray struck the faces of anyone near the bow. Excitement and foreboding swirled about in equal measure.

The bombardment of Fort Oswego began on May 5th. The ships manoeuvred themselves into a line to deliver a splendid broadside against the hopelessly outmatched defenders. The sound of nearly a hundred guns was deafening; the thundering noise constant. Our ship shuddered with each volley. Some round shot thumped into the earthen work hills placed to protect the base, but most battered the wooden walls of the fort, smashing them and whoever was inside to pieces. It was an awesome display of naval power. Unfortunately, before we shock troops were able to disembark, nature conspired with the enemy. The wind direction changed. Blowing from the south now, it pushed our ships back from shore. Our good ships were buffeted by a raging rainstorm. Not all the men were able to shelter in the small, confined space below decks. My company was forced to huddle beneath tarps that shielded us somewhat from the elements. Eventually we grew weary of standing and sat. The water that slid across the decking soaked our boots and pants. The chill night air added to our discomfort. We awaited dawn and relief from nature's counterattack.

Our assault resumed the following morning. The cool breezes and the dampness of our clothes made us even more desirous of activity that would distract us from our anxiety. We piled into small landing craft that propelled us toward the beach. The Royal Marines and some de Wattevilles, a Swiss regiment newly arrived from Europe, aimed for the fort itself. Their little craft did not land, but turned a few yards from the gravelled shore for a hasty return for reinforcements. Men were expected to wade the short distance. Underestimating the deceptive depths of Lake Ontario forced the redcoats into four feet of frigid water. Those that held their muskets high salvaged at least one shot, but their flooded cartridge pouches would provide no more. As they assembled on the beach, for some unknown reason two companies of bluecoat regulars exited any shelter that the fort might still provide and formed up in a single line atop the gentle hill that separated the redcoats from Oswego. If their intent was to repulse our troops, the plan was ill-conceived. The redcoats formed into broad columns, fixed bayonets, and like a battering ram punched great holes in the American lines.

To the west great boatloads of sailors armed with familiar boarding pikes, intent on havoc, skirted the fort and headed up-river bound for the warehouses in the little town hiding behind the fort.

My company's goal was to secure the densely wooded area on the high ground that overlooked the fort, perhaps fifty or sixty feet above the lake level. Having witnessed the Royal Marine landing I forced my oarsmen closer to shore and ordered muskets and cartridge boxes held high. Following my lead all fifty-eight green jackets pounded down the beach and ascended the broadest path on the sandy hill to the east as quickly as it would allow. When we burst onto the high ground I was startled by a squad of militiamen, half-concealed in trees about twenty yards back, levelling their muskets directly at us. "Down!" I screamed as I plunged to the sandy path. The vanguard of my men obeyed and did just that as an explosion of musket fire greeted us. My shoulder stung; my ear as well. There were yelps and groans about me. Knowing that another explosion would follow in thirty seconds I bounded up and directed this first group into skirmishing position, some to the left of the path, others to the right. "Skirmish position. On one knee. When they poke their noses out again, shoot them off." While these men spread out, I hollered back to the second squad still hidden by the earthen slope, "Conceal yourselves until the next exchange of fire. Then rush the woods. Show them your bayonets!" There was more chatter from muskets. The second squad charged forward with fury and ferocious yells. The bravest militiamen stood their ground, fought, and died. The rest, no doubt realizing they were out numbered and remembering they had homes to return to, turned and fled. My Glengarries gave chase through the woods with branches and boughs scratching and slashing, but were unable to keep pace. Having gained the high ground, I looked down to the fort and town below. From this vantage point I could see that redcoats possessed all.

By late afternoon Colonel Harvey had come in search of me, finding me not far from the spot where the Americans had attempted to kill us, with a box of cigars of the type only gentlemen could afford, tucked under one arm.

"FitzGibbon! Well done. Commend your men. General Drummond is pleased. Your area is secured?"

"Thank you, Colonel. I'll be sure to convey the General's sentiments. The lads will appreciate them. Piquets are set. The men are watching for any sign of activity. You'll be alerted if the Yankees are planning any counter-attack. It seems unlikely though."

"Casualties?"

"None dead. Nine wounded. They've been taken back to the ships for attention."

"Good. Less than one hundred all told, killed or wounded." Then staring at my left shoulder he asked, "Are you injured yourself, Captain?"

Not until that moment did I notice the small red stain upon the shoulder of my new jacket and the jagged vertical tear that ran down the sleeve from near the stain to to the elbow, damage that must have been done as I plunged forward. Suddenly I became more conscious of my aching ear. "I've suffered most grievous injury: my jacket is in need of serious repair and it's not even paid for!"

Harvey chuckled. Then focusing his gaze upon the cigar box I held, enquired: "Anything else to report?"

"Yes Sir. Cheese."

"Pardon."

"Cheese."

"What about it?"

"A great hoard of the stuff is in the farm building on the other side of the woods."

"Bring it back. All we seem to have acquired is food. Two thousand, four hundred barrels tallied so far. Everything you can imagine: flour, pork, bread, salt. Only seven small guns and some ship's rigging are here for confiscation. Whether our intelligence was incorrect or we have mistimed this venture, we do not know. Perhaps the guns we sought have not yet arrived or have already departed."

"At least we'll be well nourished and the bluecoats will go hungry."

"Some consolation." Continuing to stare at the cigar box, he repeated his question, "Anything else?"

"Yes Sir. Some militia officer seems to have abandoned these. Would you be kind enough to present these cigars to General Drummond with the compliments of the Glengarries? It's not a full box unfortunately, but the supply is still quite adequate."

Taking my offering, Harvey replied, "I assure you that the General will appreciate the gesture. As I imagine you already know, the man does enjoy a good smoke after his evening meal."

Stories did swirl in barracks. Harvey hadn't revealed anything I didn't know. And distracted as I was by my duties, I could hardly be faulted for forgetting that half the contents of the box were safely stored in my sergeant's knapsack. It was only coincidence that the number of safely secured cigars and the number of men in my company were identical.

Continuing Harvey said, "We are about to torch the warehouses and the remnants of the fort. When you see the flames, return to the beach to be picked up. The ships sail at dawn."

And so we did. Settled back on the ships we were able to watch the glorious dawn and reflect upon our adventure. Once relief and contentment had washed over me, more serious matters invaded my thoughts. My ear throbbed like I'd been stung by a monstrous bee, and the possibility of my demise flitted through my mind. I began to wonder if death stalks its victims, or merely stumbles upon them unannounced. If luck keeps a man alive, how great a portion of mine remained? Until I was able to imagine a life with Mary Haley, such things had never been considered.

# 29
## *Lundy's Lane, July 1814*

Jubilation! No better word could describe the mood on the ships as we sailed to Niagara. News from Europe was the cause of our rejoicing. Wellington and his allies were finally triumphant. The French were vanquished. Bonaparte had abdicated and been exiled. Britain's European armies would surely be on their way to North America to confront the United States. Reinforcements were coming. The only uncertainty was when and where. Both above and below decks there was unending speculation about what blows might inflict the greatest damage, and how the Americans should be punished for the offence of their invasion. Some even suggested that burning their government buildings in Washington, as they had done in York, would be fair retribution. But when we reached Fort George our optimism was immediately doused by word of General Phineas Riall's terrible defeat at Chippawa by a much improved blue coated, and now grey-jacketed, American army encamped at Queenston. Once again Upper Canada was in imminent danger.

At Fort George Lieutenant-General Gordon Drummond assumed command of the British and Canadian forces from Riall. By all accounts, Drummond accepted the Chippawa calamity stoically and went about preparing for his campaign.

We had accompanied him on the latter part of his voyage and there had been much quiet discussion among officers about the General. Those who knew Drummond regarded him most favourably. Quebec-born, he had been battle-hardened in Holland, Egypt, and the Caribbean. Like Brock, he inspired confidence, but was said to have little of Brock's charm. Habitually he wore a string of Indian beads about his neck for all to see. Apparently he was a man who believed in sending clear messages. Weary of citizens who aided and abetted the enemy, in May Drummond ordered fifty Upper Canadians charged with sedition. Treason trials were held in the little village of Ancaster in a hotel confiscated from a member of Willcocks' Canadian Volunteers. Of the nineteen in custody, fifteen were convicted: eight were hung on Burlington Heights, and seven banished to Australia, where ever that was. He'd made the consequences of disloyalty evident to all. When he gathered his officers together to outline his battle plan, he got straight to the point. "We will drive them out of Niagara; we'll push them back all the way to Buffalo. That we will. When I call upon you, I expect every man to do his part. Ready yourselves." And then we were dismissed. We relayed what he'd said to the men.

Drummond's planning required information. Was it true that the Americans had unexpectedly departed Queenston? Where had they gone? Why had they gone? What was the current strength of the American force? What were they up to? Gathering the answers was the assignment given to me and my company.

Upon settling my livery bill—basically returning to the army a goodly portion of my last pay—I retrieved Guard from the stables at Fort George and set off along the River Road at the head of my men. When we reached Queenston we found it abandoned but noticed blackish smoke billowing into the air from the direction of St. David's, the nearby village. Anxious to discover the cause, perhaps recklessly I left my men and rode off to ascertain for myself. Nearing the site, I approached with more caution and from the cover of the forest and observed what I'd expected to see: St David's, in its entirety, fully ablaze. Yet there was no one rushing about with buckets of water attempting to extinguish the flames. Whether the inhabitants had been pushed out long ago, or had given up all hope of saving their homes, I could not tell. Just as I was about to retrace my path and return to my men I heard angry shouts and the click of cocking muskets.

"Halt!"

"Don't turn round."

"Extend your arms; hold them out from your sides."

"Reach for a pistol or that sword and one of us will send you to meet your Maker."

Thoughts darted through my mind. Four separate voices: were there more men than this? Did they hold rifles or muskets? At such close range did it matter? Was this to be another embarrassment like my capture in Holland, which I vowed to myself would never happen again? Was this the occasion to chance escape and risk my life, just to avoid imprisonment?

"Did you not hear?" yelled the gruffest voice.

"Aye" said I. Slowly I extended my arms as instructed. From the rustling of nature's debris on the ground I heard one set of footsteps coming forward.

"Don't move." Then after a short pause, "FitzGibbon?"

Was the man's knowing my name to my advantage or not? Perhaps I was someone sought after like Chapin had been for me, a fugitive with a bounty on his head?

"FitzGibbon? What army do green jackets serve? Where's your redcoat?"

A husky, bearded militiaman, whom I did not recognize, with musket levelled at my stomach, moved to the front of me.

"Who are you with?' I asked with as much calmness as I could muster.

"Lincoln Militia. Those are our farms and livelihoods that you are watching go up in smoke."

I exhaled and replied, emphasizing my accent rather than softening it as I usually did. "James FitzGibbon it is. Captain of His Majesty's Glengarry Light Fencibles. Much relieved to meet you. I thought American scavengers had discovered me." Nodding in the direction of the once prosperous village I asked, "What happened?" Only when the others began to lower their weapons and cluster around, and their leader began the story, did I lower my arms.

The burly militiaman replied, "The enemy sent out foraging parties from Queenston. They scoured the area, stealing anything they could eat. Some groups were guided by Willcocks' men. We Lincolns ambushed them, and harassed them whenever they plundered our farms. Eventually they gave up and left, but decided some repayment was due. You see the result." He turned and stared toward what had been a fine, little community.

"I'm sorry for your misfortune," was all I could say. "Do you know where the bluecoats are now?"

"No. Tell Drummond when you see him, once we've seen to our families, we'll be ready."

"Aye. He'll be counting on you."

Upon returning to my company we pushed on past Queenston Heights and along the road that overlooked the gorge crafted by the river and time in search of our quarry. As we approached the Falls, the ever present roar of the water as it plunged off the escarpment could be heard and the vaporous clouds could be seen. Spray settled on our faces and clothes. My Glengarries, being from the eastern part of the province, had never experienced anything such as this. They were awed. Knowing that some of them might never witness such as this again, I let them creep to the edge of Table Rock to better observe. The bright light from the summer sun was piercing the mist to reveal an array of colours in the azure sky.

Incomparable amounts of the waters from the great, inland lakes tumbled down from the height, became a swirling torrent, and as white-capped waves jostled with one another as they raced through the gorge for their next home. It was majestic. Sublime. Nature displayed her dreadful power for all to see. To me it was a glorious, holy place, not much different from the way it had been at Creation. My mesmerized men remained motionless, mist drenching their uniforms until I called them away. Returning to our task, we marched up Lundy's Lane past several well-established farms to the Portage Road heading toward Chippawa, three miles away. As we journeyed it was most discomforting to think of the atrocity of war about to occur so close to such beauty.

Past the Widow Willson's Tavern we encountered and lightly engaged the piquets of the American army. Everything I'd discovered about the enemy was relayed back to General Drummond.

On July 25th Drummond brought his army to Lundy's Lane, the best position to defend against the larger American force. The lane itself was a slightly sunken roadway, about a mile in length, that traversed a sandy ridge, perhaps half a mile wide, rising away from the Falls. On this warm, mid-summer day the peach and cherry trees lining the road were abundant with fruit near ripening and provided ample shade. Toward Chippawa the ground sloped away from the ridge in long and gradual fashion; in the other direction, toward Queenston Heights, the grade was much sharper, providing shelter from the enemy guns and watchful eyes. The commanding view overlooking luxuriant fields of wheat and a stand of chestnut trees in the distance was from a small cemetery laid out next to a log church or meeting house. It was there that Drummond placed his guns: two large, two small, and a howitzer along with his new rocket detachment. The enemy would surely come to the cemetery; this would be the killing ground.

The entire Glengarry Regiment occupied the right flank, furthest from the Falls. Next to us were the 104th, New Brunswick lads, and the 103rd. Nearer the cemetery, the centre of our line, were the pride of the British army, red-coats: the 1st, known as the Royal Scots, that had suffered at Chippawa, the 89th, Morrison's men that had distinguished themselves at Crysler's Farm, the remnants of the 41st from Moraviantown and Chippawa wanting to prove their worth, and the 8th, known as the King's Regiment, the ones that had fought so valiantly at Stoney Creek. Behind them were the small cavalry groupings: the 19th Dragoons and Hamilton Merritt's mounted militiamen. Between the cemetery and the Falls were Norton's Grand River warriors and those who'd fought with Tecumseh, all of whom had fought savagely at Chippawa against the Seneca warriors recruited by the blue-coats, and the Upper Canadian militias, Loyalists mostly, many from Lincoln not far from where we stood. All tough men not easily moved.

Throughout the day we waited, savouring the warmth of the summer sun, tickled by breezes and lulled by the distracting sound of the Falls. Secretly we hoped we'd live long enough to enjoy another day such as this tomorrow.

About a half hour before sunset grey jackets appeared from the copse of chestnut trees. They were in column formation, in impressive numbers, and moved across the fields with deter-mination, climbing over frail fences that would not hold them back, trampling crops. Riall at Chippawa might have mistaken them for militiamen, but we knew what they were: trained, professional soldiers, the best the United States Army had. Too far away to hear, I imagined fifers urging them forward with a jaunty version of 'Yankee Doodle'. Eventually they stopped where the slope began, unfurled their flags, the eagle on navy and the regimental on beige, and staring forward awaited their next command.

While the Americans stood still, from the cemetery our artillery commenced a relentless and most destructive fire upon their position. Canisters burst in air above the tightly packed formations, spraying metal down as near to the officers and the colour bearers as the gunners could manage. As if to prove their courage the Americans remained where they were, and withstood the barrage, sustaining heavy casualties. Then in the dying light when I thought the grey jackets could suffer no more, to the beat of the drums they began their ascent of the slope, aiming themselves directly at the little graveyard.

To the left of this advance on our right flank, skirmishers advanced in the diminishing light, no doubt to assess our strength and resolve. Three companies of Glengarries, mine included, were sent to engage and drive them back. Firing independently, often from one knee we, green jackets descended in pairs, one at the ready while the other reloaded. Banks of clouds obscured the moon, making it most difficult to see our fellow combatants as things progressed. Whenever a band of starlight poked through exposing us, muskets would crackle, and crackle again as long as memory of the opponent's last muzzle flash remained. Grunts and cries would confirm if we had hit our mark or not. When the shapes in the darkness disappeared I ordered my men back to our original position. Nearing our line we were suddenly raked by musket fire from above. Something pierced my shako, knocking it to the ground. The soldier beside me lurched forward. Yelps and yells were all about. Using every curse I'd ever heard I was able to communicate the error of their ways to the jackasses who'd mistaken us for enemy, before they fired again. No later apologies from them could make amends for the unnecessary wounds they'd inflicted.

The battle was most intense at the crest of the ridge where the 89th, 1st, and 41st were placed. The fighting sounded fierce and most desperate. The furious fire of muskets, the thud of musket butts into unyielding flesh and bone, the clash of swords, the clank of bayonets on whatever attempted to block their thrust, all could be heard. Battle cries and wails of anguish accompanied the choking, acrid smoke that drifted onto us, blinding us further. Occasionally muzzle flashes would reveal silhouettes in mortal combat amidst the grave markers, but as British and American uniforms in outline were so similar and jacket colour indiscernible beyond a few feet it was impossible to tell which side was faring better. We Glengarries could do nothing except brace ourselves against the sickening smell of powder, listen, and await new orders that never arrived.

In time only muffled sounds could be heard. One side had been dislodged from the high ground. Subsequent counter-attacks came from the slope of the hill on the Queenston side. Not a good sign. Each redcoat charge to retake the guns in the graveyard was ferocious and brief, followed by silence and another attempt. Three times this happened. By midnight they charged no more and the shroud of victory settled over the little cemetery. It appeared the Americans had prevailed.

During the stillness afterwards, the lamentations of the wounded—their calls for water to quench their thirst, for relief from their misery, even for forgiveness for past sins—added to our disquiet.

At dawn as the slight chill of the night gave way, our sight was restored. To our astonishment the Americans were gone. For some unfathomable reason in the darkest night they had abandoned the high ground they'd held so dearly and disap-peared, returning the way they had come with their wounded, leaving our cherished guns behind. Only the carnage and the debris remained.

Once again my company was among those assigned the responsibility of clearing the field. We moved amidst bodies sprawled atop one another; coats of red, grey, and blue were intermingled. There were skulls shattered by sabre and musket butt, bodies gouged by ball and bayonet, lifeless faces marred with black powder grimacing in disbelief. There were the dead and nearly dead wheezing until breath forsake them. Carcasses of animals punctured by shot and torn in half by rocket lay about. In one spot horses had been dragged into line to form a lifeless rampart for men to kneel behind. Everywhere scattered about were damaged gun carriages, wheel less and overturned ammunition waggons, fractured fences, and broken crosses that not long ago had marked the graves of loved ones. Hurriedly we searched for the living. Flies swarmed about; the smell of blood had already lured them to this place. We removed our wounded to the surgeons' tents, leaving those with head and stomach injuries toward the back until those more likely to survive could be treated. British and Canadian dead were placed in common graves close to the little cemetery. Having retrieved our own casualties and buried our dead, the lifeless enemy left behind needed to be disposed of quickly. The mid-day sun was intensifying the foul smell of decay; it stung our nostrils. A trench was dug in the sandy soil and tree branches thrown in for a funeral pyre. Respectfully we placed these fallen fellow soldiers in the pit. As we did so a renegade warrior was noticed. Earlier other warriors had prowled the battlefield for their prizes, the para-phernalia of war that the dead Americans would no longer require; there was no harm in that. They had all departed with their new belongings, but this one remained. Coveting a pair of fine leather boots, he struggled to remove them from some bluecoat officer. A hoarse yell caught our attention. The young officer was not quite dead. He began to kick and made a final effort to prevent his boots from being taken. The renegade, red stripes on his forehead and charcoal ones down his cheeks, must have grown tired because he pulled a knife, stabbed the bluecoat, dragged him to the pyre and tossed him in. All but one of us stood aghast at such indignity. A shot rang out. The native clutched his chest and tumbled into the pyre beside his foe. No one sought his assailant; no reproach was attempted. The sickly smell of burning flesh filled the air.

This battlefield will long be remembered for the courage and character, for the valour and sacrifice of the men who fought and died here. And so it should. But I will never forget the slaughter I beheld that morning on Lundy's Lane.

In subsequent days losses were tallied. One quarter of Drummond's brave force was casualty. Nearly nine hundred in all. The 89th, 1st, and 8th Regiments suffered greatly. Only fifty-six Glengarries were killed or wounded. The Americans appeared to have lost equal number. We knew how many had gone into the blaze; Winfield Scott's grey jackets were most numerous. The Widow Willson said sixty uncovered waggons filled with wounded had past her tavern on the morning of the 26th. An additional eighty prisoners were taken and sent to holds of ships anchored for this purpose in Halifax harbour.

Both sides laid claim to victory. The Americans said they'd captured the hill and repelled all counter-attacks before retreating. Drummond had possession of the hill. Those of us who were there recognized Lundy's Lane for what it was: a stalemate. Anyone foolish enough to think about it knew that sorrow could be apportioned equally.

# 30
## *Kingston, August 1814*

Colonel Harvey was seated at a crudely fashioned desk outside of his tent beneath a tree laden with ripe peaches when I approached him. He was deeply engrossed in some report he was writing. It reminded me of tasks I'd once completed for General Brock. Harvey did not notice me until I stood to attention before him. His greeting was warm.

"Ahh, FitzGibbon. Always a pleasure to see you. You are looking fit and well. Good. What can I do for a man in His Majesty's Service?"

"I have a favour to ask."

"Go on. What is it?"

"I wish to convey your next military dispatch to Kingston."

Frown lines began to appear around his mouth. He lowered his pen and slowly rubbed the fingers of his left hand along his jaw line. "Let me understand this. In the midst of our planning for what may be the decisive campaign of the war, you wish to leave the front?'

"I do. It's most important. I'll return promptly, without delay."

"You must admit: it's a most unusual request. A less capable officer could easily do the job. Is there a reason for your petition?"

"Yes Sir. There is a wedding that requires my presence."

"A wedding! Whose?"

"Mine."

Seeing the humour in this, Harvey laughed and replied, "You surprise me, FitzGibbon. Wouldn't have thought you getting married would have such urgency." Then he leaned forward indicating to me that at least some elaboration was expected.

"I wish to ensure that Miss Haley will receive a widow's pension from the army should anything happen to me."

Perplexed, he said, "Those words reveal none of your characteristic confidence. Forget any premonitions you may be having. It does no good to give credence to such matters. Clear thinking and courage always win the day." He studied me carefully for a few moments, then asked, "Is there another reason?" When he recognized that no response was coming, he continued, "Perhaps there is, but I suspect I'll never know. Keeping your true intentions hidden seems much more like you. Anything else?"

"No, Sir."

"Permission granted. Be ready to leave within the hour, as soon as I finish this," he said glancing down at his papers. "Return with haste. Don't doddle. Be back before the fighting is renewed."

"You have my word, Colonel. Thank you."

Within a few days, on August 14th to be precise, Mary and I stood before the youthful Reverend Stewart arrayed in modest vestments in the simple Church of England that the Haleys attended faithfully each Sunday. Morning sunlight streamed through the windows at the front, one on each side of the finely crafted wooden altar, illuminating our spot. Cloaked in shadow in the pews were our witnesses: Mary's father William so proud of his daughter that he might burst the buttons on his suit, the amiable widow he had recently begun to court, and Mary's brother Ethan tucked behind his father. The vicar addressed us all in a most soothing voice.

"In accordance with the dictates of the Church, the Banns of Marriage have been read from the pulpit for all to hear. No one has come forward, but on this wedding day I will ask once more. If anyone here present knows of any cause of just impediment why these two persons should not be joined together in holy Matrimony, ye are to declare it." As he stared first at us and then looked to the pews, I thought how unnecessary and half-hearted this was. Mary had grown up in this small community. How impossible it would have been for her to conceal some previous marriage. And not a soul who knew anything about my life before I'd appeared on the doorstep of The Loyalist a year and a half ago had been consulted. Hearing no objection, the vicar proceeded, reading from the cherished book that he had surely brought with him from Britain. "Dearly beloved, we are gathered together here in the sight of God, and in the face of this congregation, to join together this Man and this Woman in holy Matrimony, which is an honourable estate..."

While he spoke I could not take my eyes from Mary. She was a vision in blue, the loveliest woman I could imagine. Better than I deserved. The dress that she must have laboured over many an evening by oil lamp accented the colour and sparkle of her eyes. Its fitted bodice over the full skirt favoured her figure. In her luxuriant, copper-coloured hair there was a band of fabric that matched the dress perfectly. I felt shabby in my Glengarry uniform, despite having brushed it within an inch of its life.

"...and this holy estate should be entered into reverently, discretely, advisedly, soberly, and in the fear of God." After explaining the causes for which marriage was ordained, at last he turned to his left and spoke directly to me. "James, wilt thou have this Woman to be thy wedded Wife? Wilt thou love her, comfort her, honour and keep her in sickness and in health, and forsaking all others, keep only unto her, so long as ye both shall live?"

I hesitated for an instant, not because I was unwilling to make these promises, but because I still could not believe I was being permitted to make such commitments, and said, "I will."

Turning to his right, the vicar asked Mary nearly the same question: "Wilt thou take this Man to be thy wedded Husband?" with a few words about obeying and serving thrown in. I held my breath until she said, "I will."

Holding hands we pledged our troth, each of us vowing to have and to hold from this day forward, for better or worse, for richer for poorer, in sickness and in health, to love and to cherish, till death do us part according to God's holy ordinance. I slipped the plain, metal band that had been her mother's upon Mary's finger, and promised to endow my wife with all my worldly goods, hoping that someday I'd have more than a sabre, a pistol, and a horse to share. Finally, our gentle minister pronounced us Man and Wife, advising listeners that no man should put asunder this pairing that God hath joined together. Unfortunately, the enemy was out of earshot; I would have liked them to hear as they were the ones who'd be attempting to kill me every day that remained in this bloody war.

Following the ceremony the six of us, warmed by the summer sun, travelled by foot along the dusty laneways between the church and Haley's inn. It was not long before we were heading a lively procession. Countless children, abandoning games and chores, came from the houses and cottages that lined out path. Gleefully girls in bare feet danced about offering Mary the yellow-centred white daisies that grew in their mothers' gardens. Boys, hopeful some edible treat might come their way, cheered and waved their straw hats in the air. One girl of about ten years of age coaxed a goat pulling a cart carrying two young ones to follow. Someone banged a pot with a wooden spoon. Dogs of all sorts, excited by the commotion, pranced along barking joyfully. Women folk in aprons hearing the noise stopped their work and came forward to compliment the bride and offer best wishes as she passed. An old man who'd been sitting on a bench resting his chin on the handle of a cane, rose and tipped his hat to me. All told, nothing could have been more splendid.

Mary's father had closed The Loyalist to custom for the day, but it was still filled to overflowing. Friends and neighbours of the Haleys greeted us. Men with jars of beer and cider in their hands toasted us and slapped me on the back in congratulations. Women clustered about Mary complimenting her on the dress she'd made and said how beautiful she looked. I could not have agreed more. Savoury aromas escaped through the open windows from the abundant food laid out in the dining room, generously provided by the guests. Two fiddlers, father and son by the look of them, wandered about entertaining everyone with their tunes, adding to the festive atmosphere.

When those outside in the courtyard were summoned for the meal Mary and I were at last alone. She kissed me gently. I could see mischief in those eyes. "You are far too handsome, James FitzGibbon. Young ladies will be throwing themselves at you. You'll need to beware. Is there nothing you can do about your appearance?"

"I'll see what I can do. There is only one woman I'd be wanting to throw herself at me."

"And whom would that be?"

"Forgotten her name I have, but you'd know the one I mean. The one with the copper- coloured hair and the entrancing blue eyes."

"I think I do know the one you mean: the intelligent, good-natured one who turns the head of every young man she meets?"

"That's the one. Unless she's got an identical twin, I'll never be tempted by another. Do you think she has?"

"Not that I've noticed. Are you serious about her then?"

"I am. I dream about her. In fact, I even dreamt that I married her this morning. I feared that when I woke she'd be gone."

"No fear of that. She's always dreamed of marrying a handsome soldier, and dreams do come true."

Seeing no one observing, Mary kissed me passionately. Then she asked, "Husband, do you know the secret of a happy marriage?"

"Tell me."

"It's dress colour, according to the tales. 'Marry in blue and he'll always be true'. Widening her skirt in a curtsey so I'd get a better look, she added, "You'll see I'm not taking any chances. I'm following the advice. I must admit I was tempted to choose a delicate, fawn-coloured fabric that I much admired, but 'Marry in brown and you'll live out of town."

"Would you not be content with that? I don't know what the future holds for us. Until this war is over it will be best for you to remain here with your father. Afterwards we'll have a better sense of my prospects."

"All that matters is that we are together."

The next morning I was on a ship bound for Niagara, watching Kingston harbour grow smaller and disappear, clutching a satchel of papers for Harvey and General Drummond.

# 31
## *Fort Erie, September 1814*

My promise to Colonel Harvey could not be kept; fighting on the Niagara resumed before I returned.

To deliver the dispatches to Harvey, I had to find him. Neither he nor the army were where I expected them to be. The new encampment was at the far end of Niagara about a mile or two from Fort Erie. I found it in considerable distress. Beneath the branches of trees offering shade sat disconsolate soldiers with bandaged eyes and heads, next to men with white cloth bound around stumps that had once been limbs. Flaps of countless tents were tied back to let in air. Flies swarmed above the wounded laying inside. Militiamen guided horse-drawn waggons filled with the remains of men bound for mass graves. Soldiers strong enough to stand shuffled past giant black caldrons where cooks ladled the mushy contents onto plates. A fatigued John Harvey stood in the midst of all this conversing with a bare-headed surgeon, sleeves rolled up, still wearing a blood-spattered apron, exhaustion etched on his young face. As I dismounted and approached the Colonel, the surgeon glanced in my direction before departing. I could think of no suitable words of comfort to offer him.

"Sir, what's happened?"

Harvey closed his eyes for a moment, took a deep breath and began to recount the story. "Several days ago we attempted to take Fort Erie. Do you know it?"

"I do. Star-shaped, stone structure on the edge of Lake Erie. Been awhile since I've seen it."

"You won't recognize it now. The Americans have dug earthen embankments from the the fort on the river's edge all along the lakefront to the place called Snake Hill to the west. Wooden spikes and sharpened branches protect the top."

"The Americans have had sufficient time for their constructions. Since Lundy's Lane."

"They have, but General Drummond intends to do whatever is necessary to push them from Upper Canada. Perhaps the plan was too ambitious: a four pronged assault at night. Things went wrong from the start. The native warriors' diversion was ill-timed. The attack of the De Watteville Regiment on the Snake Hill battery failed; the damned scaling ladders brought for the walls were too short. The attack by the 103rd on the left flank faltered when their colonel, Hercules Scott, fell mortally wounded. Colonel William Drummond's charge with the 104th was our only hope of success. The 104th triumphed, capturing the old stone buildings, but then the powder magazine underneath blew up. The explosion shook the earth; we could feel violent tremors beneath our feet. Fire lit up the sky long enough for us to see mangled bodies, timber, and stone catapulted into the air. Hundreds of tons of black powder must have ignited."

"Casualties were heavy?" I asked, although I knew the answer simply by looking about.

Harvey nodded affirmatively. "Worse than Lundy's Lane. One quarter of General Drummond's force; nine hundred men are dead, wounded, or missing. I don't know what our official report will say, but it's a bloody catastrophe. I don't see how we can continue this siege."

Yet continue the siege we did.

Glengarries were not involved in the assault; the green jackets had been held in reserve and suffered little in comparison . Things changed: during the siege we played a central part. To defend the British-Canadian position and protect the heavy artillery that pounded the American fort daily we served as piquet in the mile deep forest than surrounded Fort Erie. We were expected to keep enemy foraging parties from venturing out in search of provisions, stop excursions to probe the strength of our defences, and at all costs, protect the guns that added misery to their republican lives. In rotation the entire regiment was involved. So too were John Norton's warriors. For hours on end we'd huddle in small gullies, behind trees ancient before any of us were born, in thickets of saplings and dense clumps of brush, behind boulders deposited by mysterious force. Then we'd wait until intruders stumbled into our lair. Sometimes a day or two would go by without any activity and long periods of boredom gave the men too much time to think.

For the first two weeks, our assignment could best be described as unenviable. The autumn weather, arriving far too early, made it worse. The rain was incessant—thirteen days in a row. Deluges alternated with drizzle. On the few occasions when it did neither, thick mist obscured our view and droplets of moisture dripped from the leaves and branches above. Sodden earth quickly turned into oozing mud that gripped feet and knees and buttocks if a man was foolish enough to sit and rest. Rain seeped through disintegrating boots and soaked tattered wool uniforms that offered little comfort from the night air. To keep our powder dry and serviceable, hands needed to be cupped over musket's pan and flint. Muscles ached from crouching. Occasionally dappled light would pierce the gloom, but mostly there were shadows. We'd strain our ears listening for breaks in the stillness: the rustle of leaves, the snap of twigs. We'd stare intently searching for the flash of white pants beneath branches; we'd watch at shoulder height for the sway of boughs. When the enemy did enter the killing ground a few yards before us, we'd burst from our hiding places to fire muskets into disbelieving faces or stick them with bayonets, twisting to ensure the gaping hole would never heal.

Day after wretched day this continued: killing men we'd never met, even might have liked if we'd known them in a different time, praying that we'd be quick and lucky enough to prevent them from doing the same to us.

The brief periods of relief we were given did little to improve our spirits. Mud engulfed the camp as well. Tents provided protection from the rain, but were pitched on saturated ground. Damp blankets could not keep the chill at bay. The rain doused camp fires. None of us could remember a warm, satisfying meal. Sleep eluded all but the truly exhausted. Sickness and sullenness spread.

More than a month after the initial assault, General Drummond finally relented. He ordered his army back to Chippawa; the siege was brought to an end. If he'd waited much longer the roads would have been impassable and horses would never have been able to pull the artillery pieces through the rivers of mud. Glengarries and native warriors were instructed to provide rearguard protection during the withdrawal.

Perhaps it was just coincidence. More likely the Americans sensed our departure and launched their strongest sortie yet. The fighting in the forest was fierce. We attempted to delay the bluecoat advance while our redcoats made their escape. Every manoeuvre we'd practised was employed. My Glens withdrew in pairs, moving at angles, not straight back making enemy aim easier. Fixing eyes on some protective tree or stump, hidden by covering clouds of musket smoke, they'd dart to the new position, staying only long enough for one man to select a target and the second to reload. For safety the pairs kept their distance from one another; it was dangerous to bunch up giving enemy marksmen broader targets. I endeavoured to control the movement so we could move back in unison though the unevenness of the terrain and the obstacles in the wood made this difficult. We barely kept twenty or thirty yards ahead of our pursuers. Too late I saw a bluecoat's musket pointed at me. Something thumped into my chest, staggering me backwards. On the ground I waited for the searing pain that surely must come. Seconds passed with less pain than I'd imagined. Shock began to set in, dulling my thinking. Was this what dying was like: life quietly slipping away before even comprehending what was happening? As my eyes began to close two figures in green placed a shoulder under each arm and dragged me off.

When I did open my eyes again, the same weary surgeon who'd been speaking with Harvey when I first arrived, knelt beside me. "Ahh! You're awake. Good man. I'm Surgeon William Dunlop of the 89th: 'Tiger' Dunlop to my friends." Chuckling to himself, he added, "Come to think of it, it's 'Tiger' Dunlop to my enemies as well. What's your name?"

"FitzGibbon."

"Right. I thought it was. Good that you still remember it. Two of your men rescued you. They're gone now. Where were you hit?"

I patted my chest where it throbbed the most.

"There's no hole in your jacket, nor blood that I can see. Let's open up this jacket and shirt of yours." After his inspection he added, "I can find only a darkening bruise that's growing. You've received a heavy blow."

"Why am I not dead?" I stammered.

"Your rescuers said that the musket ball passed through a young sapling, cutting it in two, before getting to you." Smiling, he continued, "I've heard it said that the devil tries to take the good men first, so there will be more of the rest to do his work here on earth. If that's true you must be one hell of a soldier, FitzGibbon, to still be alive. Come on," he said helping me to my feet. "I'll take you back with me. I've ordered your

rescuers to tell your company that the job is done, with con-
spicuous bravery, and they should pull back to Chippawa as
well. My 89th is the last regiment to leave."

"Thank you."

"See that bunch over there?" he asked pointing to a small
group of redcoats assembled and ready to march. "That's
what's left of my regiment: three officers and sixty men of
other ranks. We were four hundred before Crysler's Farm. If
this war doesn't end soon FitzGibbon, there will be none of
us left."

# 32
## *Fort Erie, November 1814*

From mid-September until early November nothing happened. The army of General Drummond dug in at Chippawa and braced itself for a counter-attack. The American army commanded by General Brown remained where it was within Fort Erie. Like two prize fighters, too weary to continue and too proud to leave, the armies were motionless. But both were wary. Each blast of frigid air reminded all that the Canadian winter was fast approaching. Something was likely to happen. Soon.

On November 5th Colonel Harvey summoned me to his tent. "Captain Fitzgibbon, just the man I need. I've a mission for a soldier with your talents."

"Sir?"

"Our native friends have been keeping a watchful eye on Fort Erie for us. Word has come that last night there were a number of explosions at the fort. This morning there is no sign of activity. General Drummond requires an officer to investigate and confirm this report. I've recommended you."

"Thank you, Colonel," I replied, all the while wondering how dangerous this honour would prove to be.

As if reading my thoughts, Harvey continued, "Should you find yourself in an unanticipated situation, I am confident

that you will be able to talk your way out of any difficulties."
I appreciated the sentiment, but his words did little to reduce
my trepidation.

By late afternoon I'd reached my intended destination.
From the edge of the surrounding wood, the trees now bare,
I looked through my telescope. The disappearing November
light made observation difficult. There was no obvious activity. Other than the lulling sound of the wind nothing could
be heard. Perhaps this was a deception. No true assessment
of the situation could be made without entering the fort
and seeing for myself. So with white handkerchief clearly
displayed, dangling from my sword, I proceeded cautiously.
At my gentle urging Guard ambled across the two hundred
yard clearing. One rifleman left behind would be enough to
alter my circumstance forever. While scanning the ramparts,
I attempted to calm myself and assure my pounding heart
that no escape from the chest was possible. Passing through
one of the gaping holes blown in the embankment, I entered.
Logs and sharpened logs were strewn about. Giant blocks of
stone, whole and in pieces, lay where the powder magazine
explosion had deposited them. Walls and barracks that had
taken years to construct were now rubble. The flagpole was
bare; the proud American eagle stretching its wings beneath
a small galaxy of stars in a navy sky no longer fluttered in the
breeze. Standing tall in my stirrups, I looked in all directions.
No other conclusion could be reached: they were gone.

# 33
## *York, April 1816*

Soft morning light slips through the window onto the desk in the sitting room of our small rented house in York. Except for the chattering of the birds in the yard, all is quiet. Mary, expecting our second child, rests in the bedroom next to our little one who is slumbering peacefully. There will be no better time to finish my account of the conflict now referred to as the War of 1812. Next week my new posting begins, and I shall have responsibilities.

Perhaps one day people will learn of this record and wish to read it. This would be most gratifying. However, this was not the main reason for undertaking this endeavour. My motivation has more to do with memories. I wish to preserve some and disperse others. It seems that the best memories are easily retained. I'll bump into a fellow soldier in the street and we'll reminisce; I'll meet a friend in a tavern and together we'll laugh about some incident that seems much more amusing in hindsight. These memories stay fresh but what of others? How quickly will I forget details, and lose track of events if I do not write them down? Important things I know I will not forget. Unbidden, thoughts of men I admired and considered friends—Isaac Brock, John Macdonell, Cecil Bisshopp, even Tecumseh, come to me often, and I take pleasure in remembering them. These were all men of fire and ice. From them I've learned about leadership and valour, about sacrifice, about humility and civility, and about heroism. My memory is their legacy. If this record helps me to recollect the details, the small events, then it has all been worthwhile. Then there are the images I wish to banish from my consciousness. A soldier's deeds, sights I have seen, the things that disturb my sleep and creep into my waking thoughts, these I wish to forget. By putting them to paper I hope to purge these images from my mind and reduce their effect upon me. Only time will reveal if this happens.

The War of 1812 has been over for more than a year now. The peace was negotiated in Belgium the day before Christmas in 1814. Regrettably, the result was not officially approved and announced until March of the subsequent year, too late for the thousands of redcoats buried in New Orleans' graves. According to the *York Gazette*, in the treaty the two sides agreed to 'status quo ante bellum', a Latin phrase meant to impress. I am told it means that everything is to return to the way it was before the war began. Of course, with the exception of the borders, almost nothing important is as it was, in spite of what politicians and diplomats might say. Upper Canada is different; its people have changed. Five years ago few who lived here showed much interest in who governed them. Some would joke that no one did. They saw themselves as rugged individuals, pioneers taming a less than hospitable land. No one could have spoken of common accomplishments or collective aspirations. Debate on public issues, like how war reparations should be paid or how more Britons could be enticed to immigrate, was unimaginable. Excluding the Loyalists, ill-treated in the past, few had harboured animosity toward the Americans. Forced to defend their homes and resist an invasion, circumstance has united them. Everyone recognizes that but for the redcoats, the conquest would be complete, and the King has earned their loyalty. Flirtation with republic ideals is over; that ended with the death of Joseph Willcocks at Fort Erie. Now it will take time for the people to forgive those who have trespassed against them. Perhaps it is too soon to say that those living in Upper Canada are beginning to think of themselves as a nation, the way the people of French Canada do, but I suspect it won't be long until this happens.

The native peoples still have not been given an independent homeland. John Norton tells me that all hope of that has disappeared.

As for myself, I have not returned to the way I was before. No longer do I consider war a grand adventure. In war people risk their lives and die for things they cherish. It is a last resort, not to be entered into impetuously or without great deliberation. I have seen too much death to think otherwise. Yet despite my repugnance for war, were Upper Canada to be invaded again I would return to arms. People must be able to choose the form of government they wish. No one should be permitted to impose an alien form of government upon them. No people should be held hostage by another. The safety of families must be ensured; people must be protected from harm. Citizens must stop injustice if they see it being done. These are the things we fought for in the War of 1812, and would fight for again. God grant that this may never be necessary.

The Glengarry Light Fencibles have recently been disbanded. It was always the intention of the British army to do this when the war concluded. As a pension I am to receive half a captain's pay. Friends have helped me secure a position in the office of the Adjutant- General of the Militia of Upper Canada here in York. Together the two incomes should permit my family to live modestly and me to pay down some of my debts.

As for Ireland, I doubt that I shall see that grand country again. This Canada has become my home. I will always be ready to defend her. My future lies here.

# *Author's Note*

Considerable research was done before writing *Redcoat 1812*. The portrait of early life in Upper Canada is authentic, and the account of the war that shaped the Canadian nation is truthful. James FitzGibbon was a real person, as were most but not all of the characters in the novel. FitzGibbon's life experiences give structure to the story, but ultimately *Redcoat 1812* is fiction—a work of my imagination. Two deliberate deviations from history should be noted. Although FitzGibbon resigned his adjutancy at the beginning of the war to rejoin the 49th Regiment and be more involved in combat, in the novel he retains his position longer to better recount events at Detroit and Queenston Heights. As well, FitzGibbon's near death experience was placed during the withdrawal from Fort Erie, rather than in 1813 for dramatic effect.

Hope you enjoyed the story.

John Nixon

CPSIA information can be obtained at www.ICGtesting.com
Printed in the USA
LVOW131224091212

310779LV00003B/407/P